"Don't do this to yourself."

"I'm not doing anything to myself. I'm doing it for them." She pointed toward the parlor.

"But you don't have to. Let me help."

Tears burned her eyes, and she shook her head. "I need to do this myself."

"Why?"

She didn't want to depend on him or anyone else. She could depend on only herself. "I just do. Please go."

He stared at her a moment before releasing her. "You are too stubborn for your own good." He yanked at his shirtsleeves to unroll them. "You are like an old mule sinking in the mud, refusing help." He marched out of the kitchen and through the parlor.

Olivia's unspent tears spilled over. She wasn't stubborn.

She was… She was…

She slapped her tears away.

She was *not* stubborn.

Mary Davis is an award-winning author of more than a dozen novels. She is a member of American Christian Fiction Writers and is active in two critique groups. Mary lives in the Colorado Rocky Mountains with her husband of thirty years and three cats. She has three adult children and one grandchild. Her hobbies are quilting, porcelain doll making, sewing, crafts, crocheting and knitting. Please visit her website, marydavisbooks.com.

Books by Mary Davis

Love Inspired Heartsong Presents

Her Honorable Enemy
Romancing the Schoolteacher
Winning Olivia's Heart

MARY DAVIS

Winning Olivia's Heart

HEARTSONG
PRESENTS

Recycling programs for this product may not exist in your area.

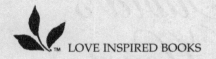 LOVE INSPIRED BOOKS

ISBN-13: 978-0-373-48783-7

Winning Olivia's Heart

Copyright © 2015 by Mary Davis

www.Harlequin.com

Printed in U.S.A.

When pride comes, then comes disgrace,
but with humility comes wisdom.
—*Proverbs* 11:2

Dedicated in loving memory of my son Josh.
I miss you.

Also to my mom, Zola, and sisters, Kath & Deb,
who tramped around the San Juan Islands with me.
It was a blast!

Chapter 1

San Juan Island, Washington, 1899

Olivia Bradshaw stopped midstride on the brick walk outside her home. She adjusted the quilt-wrapped box in her arms.

Troy Morrison leaned against the large oak tree out front. He wore a white shirt and brown trousers with a matching vest and cap. A slow smile stretched his mouth.

Her heart sped up.

Troy might very well be the most handsome man on earth. His chiseled face, deep blue eyes and dimpled smile would melt any female heart. His dark wavy hair was part tamed and part wild, just like the man. Though he worked mostly indoors at the bank, cutting wood and other physical work gave him a well-muscled body.

He pushed away from the tree. "Hello, Liv."

The problem wasn't that he was incredibly good-

looking or that women—both single and married—
fawned over him. The problem lay in his knowing that
his appearance had a devastating effect on women, yet
not understanding how it hurt her to see women flirting with him.

No, it wasn't the flirting. She understood completely
why women would flirt with him. The real problem was
that he did nothing to discourage it. He told her time and
time again that he cared naught for any woman save her.
And she told him time and time again that she didn't like
the flirting.

"Troy. I wasn't expecting to see you here." But she'd
known he'd come. And that sent a thrill through her.

He held his arms out from his sides. "Yet here I am.
You look lovely in that dress. It matches your eyes."

The very reason she had chosen this light blue cotton dress. She had hoped he'd notice. "This old thing?"

"All the men will want to spend time with you." His
gaze shifted past her to the porch, where her grandmother
stood next to Olivia's mother in her wheelchair. He doffed
his jaunty cap and gave a great sweeping bow. "Mrs.
Bradshaw, you are looking beautiful today. Granny Bradshaw, as spry as ever."

She heard Gran plant a kiss on her hand and blow it
to Troy. Olivia sighed. If Gran were fifty years younger,
she would probably run off with Troy if he would agree.

Olivia's mother spoke. "It's always good to see you,
Troy."

He chuckled. "I wish everyone in your household felt
the same."

Oh, brother. Olivia shifted her bundle again and continued walking. Her boots tapped on the bricks.

He claimed to love her. At times she believed him.
But others?

He hurried up to her. "Let me carry that for you." He reached for her quilt-wrapped box.

She swiveled and stepped around him. "Thank you, but I have it." It would be imprudent of her to allow him to carry her parcel. 'Twas the picnic box she'd made for the box social, one of the many festivities planned for this Fourth of July. She'd wrapped a quilt around it just so *he* could not see what her box looked like. It would serve him right to see her eating with some other fellow. Then he'd know what it felt like.

He stepped in front of her and wouldn't let her continue.

"Mr. Morrison, please remove yourself from my path."

"Not until you allow me to carry your burden."

She narrowed her eyes.

He narrowed his eyes back and leaned in. "I know what you have. Your supper for the auction."

"And you want to know what my box looks like."

He slapped his hand onto his chest. "I promise not to peek."

She found that hard to believe. "So you don't plan to bid on mine?" Disappointing.

"Don't worry, Liv. You'll be eating with me."

"How if you don't know what mine looks like?"

"I know you. So I'll *know* which box is yours." He snatched it from her grasp.

She gasped. "You had better not peek."

"I give you my word as a gentleman."

"That means little. You would need to be a gentleman first."

He dipped his head toward the street. "Shall we?"

She headed in that direction. "I didn't make any of your favorites."

"I like everything you cook."

He was so infuriating! They strolled down Spring Street and turned onto Second.

"When are you going to forgive me?" He glanced at her sideways.

She gazed into his deep blue eyes. The longing tugged at her. "Perhaps tomorrow."

"That's what you said yesterday and the day before that and the day before that and the day before that."

"I did not see you on Friday, so I couldn't have said it to you then."

"Oh, I'm sure you said it."

How did he know? "You think you know everything, don't you?"

"Not at all. There are a great many things I don't know. Like how deep the ocean is. Or where rainbows end." He tilted his head toward her. "Or when you're going to forgive me. But pretty much everything else about you, I do know."

He couldn't possibly.

The church came into view. People had begun to arrive. Since it was a nearly cloudless day once the morning fog had burned off, the table for the boxes stood outside along the north side of the building.

She stopped at the edge of the lawn. "I'll take that now."

He held the box away from her. "I've got it."

So he was going to peek, after all.

He strode up to the table and set the bundle down. "Miss Bradshaw's contribution." He shook Pastor Kearns's hand. "I hope the box social brings in a goodly sum of money for the school."

"It usually does." The pastor reached for the quilt. "That's quite a bundle."

Troy put his hand on top of it. "She doesn't want me to see hers. Unfair advantage." He winked.

The pastor smiled. "I see."

"Good day, Pastor." Troy turned away from the table, scooped up Olivia's hand and kissed it. "I will see you later."

She watched him go. He didn't once glance over his shoulder to see which box was hers. He met up with Nick and George, and the three went off together.

"Olivia, your quilt."

She turned to the pastor and took the quilt. "Thank you." When she turned back, Troy was gone. Disappointment tapped her on the shoulder. He didn't care. No. She was glad he hadn't seen.

"Olivia!" Felicity and her entire family marched across the grass. Felicity held a box for the social. As did her four sisters and her mother. Her youngest sister at fifteen, she was finally allowed to participate this year. The Devlins made quite the contribution with six boxes. Mr. Devlin would be sure to win his wife's.

Felicity set her box on the table and gave Olivia a hug. "Where's Troy gone off to? After what happened last year, I would think you would be keeping him close. Today of all days."

Olivia dropped her quilt in the growing pile to be used later. She looped her arm through her friend's and they strolled down the street. "He'd best behave himself. I can't watch him every minute."

"Then you've forgiven him?"

"I want to." At first, she had been too hurt to forgive him. Then her pride had kept her quiet. And then it became this game of cat and mouse. For the life of her, she couldn't figure out who was who. Sometimes she felt like the cat, and others the mouse. "I just don't know if I can trust him."

"So why are you letting him go off by himself?"

"He wasn't by himself. He was with Nick and George."

"That isn't any better."

Olivia and Felicity headed toward the games. Standing on the sidelines, she watched Troy at the starting line of the sack race. He glanced her direction and winked. The gun went off while Troy wasn't paying attention. A poor start for him. At least two hops behind everyone.

Go! Go! Hop faster! Faster!

Each of his hops was longer than anyone else's. He caught up and took the lead as he crossed the finish line. Another victory.

She clapped enthusiastically and then suddenly stopped. Did he always win at everything he did? She couldn't remember a time he hadn't.

Felicity nudged her. "I won't tell him."

She could always count on her friend. "Let's do the three-legged race."

"No. I don't want to look like a fool in front of Nick."

"Come on. It'll be fun."

Felicity folded her arms and shook her head.

A strip of cloth dangled in front of Olivia's face, and Troy spoke from behind her. "I'll be your partner. Always."

Taking her time, she swiveled around. "No, thank you."

"Come on, Liv. I know you want to. With me as your partner, you're sure to win."

A sugary voice behind Troy said, "I'll be your partner."

Violet Jones sidled up next to Troy and coiled her hands around his muscled arm.

Troy had the gall to smile at Violet. "That's right kind of you, but—"

"He already has a partner." Olivia grabbed his other arm and pulled him to the starting line. She was the cat at the moment.

His breath tickled her ear as he whispered, "You are quite lovely when you're jealous."

"You would love it if I were jealous, wouldn't you? Well, I'm not."

"Could have fooled me." He smirked and held up the cloth. "Would you do the honors?"

She tied the strip around their ankles and stood. Heat rushed through her at being so close to him.

"Put your arm around me." He hooked his around her waist without delay. "Remember to start with our tied feet first." He lifted his foot to make sure hers went with his. He reached around his back, pulled her arm around his waist, and held her hand to his hip.

She was twenty-three years old. What was she doing participating in a race? She would look the fool, as Felicity had said. But the only person's opinion she cared about was lashed to her ankle. And he was taking advantage of this opportunity to be near her. Closer than would normally be socially acceptable.

The gun sounded, and all eight teams hobbled forward.

After only one overlong step, Troy matched her gait.

Olivia wanted to finish first. If she could just lengthen her stride a little. Instead, she tripped. As she felt herself going down, she found it didn't matter if she didn't win, but Troy should.

Before she realized what he was doing, Troy tightened his hold around her waist and lifted her off the ground. "I've got you."

He certainly did. She slapped her free hand on her straw sailor hat to keep it on her head.

With her feet dangling, Troy made up the difference. Unencumbered by her shorter legs, he crossed the finish line at the same time as the lead pair.

A tie.

Troy set her feet back on the ground. "Sorry I couldn't give you a clean win, but you were still first."

He was taking the blame for them not being the sole winners when it was her who put them behind by tripping. If he would only take responsibility for real transgressions, they wouldn't have any problems.

She tried unsuccessfully to bend to untie their ankles. "I need to remove the cloth."

Troy kept his arm solidly around her. "I kind of like you being attached to me."

And just like that, he'd reduced her to the mouse. "I am not going to walk around all day like this. Now unhand me or I'll—"

"You'll what, Liv?" He smiled, flashing his dimples and perfect white teeth. "What could you possibly do?"

She couldn't think of anything, so she pinched his arm.

He laughed. "You'll have to do more than that. I have you right where I want you."

She wanted to throw a tantrum, but that would only encourage him. She hated being the mouse. She spoke in a soft, calm voice. "I don't think you do, or you wouldn't need to resort to a tether and manhandling me."

His smile faded. He crouched and untied them. He looped the cloth around her neck. "You won this time. I *will* see you later." He walked away.

She had regained her standing as the cat. But her victory left a hollow place inside her.

Felicity joined her. "I don't see why you don't just forgive him and marry him. Then all the other women would know he is taken."

"You think a wedding band would stop them from throwing themselves at him?" It hadn't stopped Widow Baxter from stealing Olivia's father. "Just because he's handsome and charming, he thinks he can do anything he wants without consequences. When will he realize some of his actions hurt others?" If she didn't love him so much, the pain wouldn't cut so deep.

"It's not his fault ladies find him irresistible."

"But he doesn't discourage them. Just once I wish he would. But he'll see what it feels like when someone else wins my box."

"You didn't tell him which box is yours?"

Olivia shook her head.

"You don't want to eat with him?"

"Of course I do. But if he has to watch me eat with another fellow, it will be worth it. Maybe he'll finally understand what I've been trying to tell him all these years."

"That means he will win someone else's box. Do you really want him eating with another girl? Especially after last year?"

Olivia recalled the image of Violet Jones in his arms, kissing him. "He doesn't have to bid on any boxes."

"A man like Troy is not going to go hungry or endure the humility of being alone." Felicity took her arm. "Want to go on a hayride before the auction?"

"That would be fun."

The Pattersons gave hay wagon rides for a penny apiece.

When Olivia and Felicity arrived, Nick, George and Troy waited their turns. Or rather Troy waited for her, Nick for Felicity, and George for Anita Patterson.

Nick and George helped their girls up into the back of the hay-filled wagon.

"Come on, Olivia," Felicity said.

Olivia stepped back. "You go on. I'm going to stay here."

Troy snagged her hand and kept her from retreating. "I've already paid your fare."

She'd known he would. And she knew he would insist. He tugged her forward and lifted her up. He hustled in behind her.

The wagon lurched, and Olivia threw out her arms to balance herself.

Troy caught her around the waist. "I've got you."

She lingered in his arms a moment. "You can let go of me now."

He leaned close to her ear. "What if I don't want to?"

Before she realized what he was doing, he pretended to lose his balance and pulled her down with him. "Oops."

Nick and George snickered.

She tried to wiggle from his grasp. "You did that on purpose."

"Did I?" He settled her in the hay next to him as the wagon rolled forward. "Admit it. You like being in my arms."

She didn't dare and straightened her hat instead.

The problem with Troy was that he made too many presumptions. And the most irritating thing about them was he was generally right.

The mouse once more. "If it weren't for the wagon jostling me about, I would extricate myself from you."

He nudged her. "Good thing I told Mr. Patterson to find the bumpiest roads he could."

Good thing.

She did enjoy being near Troy. But she couldn't let him know that, or he would be impossible. Correction, more impossible.

After the hayride, Troy escorted her to the church lawn where the auction was about to start. The single ladies gathered to one side, the single men the other. The wives who'd brought boxes stood with their husbands.

Pastor Kearns rapped a hammer on a chunk of wood lying on the table to quiet the crowd. "Remember that the money raised today will purchase a new roof and new books for the schoolhouse. So bid high." He held up the first box, yellow with a blue ribbon. "What's my bid for this lovely box? I smell apple pie."

Troy raised his hand. "A nickel." He looked at her and winked. He was insufferable.

Olivia straightened a little. That wasn't her box. Troy would end up with another lady's box right from the start. She hoped it belonged to one of the older ladies who participated just to help raise money.

Several other men bid, but Troy didn't again. Mr. Zimmerman won his wife's box.

Troy again started the bidding at a nickel. Did he really expect to win a box bidding like that? But when he opened the bidding at a nickel for the next several boxes, she knew he wasn't trying to win any of them. He was waiting. Waiting for her to give away when her box came up.

'Twas simple. She would outwit him. So when the pastor held up her red-and-black box, she acted as she had with all the other boxes.

The pastor looked straight at Troy. "Do I have an opening bid?"

Troy nodded. "Five dollars."

The crowd drew in a collective gasp.

No! He couldn't possibly know. *Someone else bid. Pleeease, someone else bid.*

Chapter 2

Troy glanced in Liv's direction. Her mouth hung open. She'd really thought he wouldn't know her box. He wasn't about to let some other fellow eat supper with her. She was his girl, even if she was too stubborn to admit it.

"Do I have another bid?" Pastor Kearns called.

The crowd stood silent a moment before Nick called out, "Give it to him!"

Then George yelled, "Yeah, it's his."

Troy knew that once he'd made a serious bid, few—if any—would venture to challenge him, knowing he usually got what he wanted. And he wanted that box. *And* the girl who went with it.

"Very well." The pastor raised the hammer to declare him the winner.

"Ten dollars," Troy said.

The pastor stared at him. "Son, you don't have to bid again. You've won the box."

Troy swaggered up to the table. "It's all for a good cause." He winked at Liv. "And well worth it." His bid would let her know how important she was to him. He held up his money. "Are you going to hit that block of wood, or should I?"

The pastor smiled as he let the hammer drop. "The town appreciates your contribution."

Troy claimed his prize, held the box up, and smiled straight at Liv. "Shock" didn't fully describe her expression. "Stricken" might cover most of the emotions flickering across her features.

Once the auction was over, each man collected the lucky—or not so lucky—lady whose box he'd won. Couples and families spread quilts out across the church lawn.

Troy offered Liv his arm. "Shall we?"

With her quilt draped over one arm, she reluctantly shoved her other hand through the crook of his elbow. "How did you know which one was mine?"

"I know you too well, Olivia Bradshaw." Nick and George had been a great help, watching the pastor unwrap it and describing it to him in detail. Then, to make sure, they'd each jabbed him surreptitiously when her box came up.

Liv kicked at the hem of her blue dress as she walked. "Why must you be so obstinate?"

"Why must you be so stubborn?" But he knew his behavior was partly to blame. And she had never seemed to get over her father passing away.

She huffed out a breath. "Look, there's a spot near Anita and George."

Poor George. To be with Anita, he had to sit with her parents and younger brothers in the center of the multitudes.

Troy guided Liv away. "I much prefer over there.

By Nick and Felicity." They were on the far edge of the grounds under a thicket of maple trees. He moved her along before she could protest. Still well within sight of everyone, just not in the middle of it all.

He set the box in the grass and took the opposite edge of her quilt. Once it was spread out, he took her hand and assisted her as she sat. He moved the box onto the quilt.

She reached for the lid.

He pulled the box onto his lap. "Uh-uh. This is mine. I paid for it."

"Oh, don't be juvenile."

He handed her the lid. "You may have that."

Her mouth twitched to contain a smile. She may think him obstinate and juvenile, but she was fond of him none-theless. And as long as he held her heart, he didn't mind this little game they played.

He removed two red-checkered napkins and then pulled out a third napkin with four biscuits wrapped in it. The butter and flour aromas delighted his nose. "You make the best biscuits." He took out two quart-size jars filled with lemonade. "I love lemonade." He removed a smaller jar. "Is this your granny's strawberry preserve? I love this." He glanced sideways at Liv.

She had her jaw set, evidently trying not to enjoy his praise of all she'd brought.

He widened his eyes. "Is this fried chicken? I love fried chicken." He pulled out the cloth-covered bowl and drew in a long breath through his nose. His mouth watered. "Are there drumsticks? I love drumsticks."

Liv struggled to hide a smile, but her crinkled eyes gave away her amusement.

He reached into the bottom of the box. "What's this?" He pulled back the cloth covering of another bowl. "I love chocolate cake." He dipped his finger in the frosting and licked it. It tasted as good as it smelled. He knew it would. "I can't imagine what would have been in here if you *had* packed my favorites."

"Just stop it. We both know they're all your favorites."

He leaned toward her. "So you *did* want me to win your box?"

"No." She folded her arms. "I wanted you to see another fellow eating all your favorite foods with me."

"Well, fortunately for me, I am the other fellow." He held the bowl out to her. "Want some of my chicken?"

She gave him a withering look before taking a fat piece.

He chose a drumstick and lounged back on one elbow. "Did you really hope I wouldn't win your box?"

"It would have been more enjoyable to see you watching from afar as another man ate your food."

That would not have been enjoyable at all. He shook his head. "I know this is all an act, Liv."

"I don't know what you're talking about."

She did, too. But he wouldn't press her into admitting it. The day was going well. He didn't want to spoil it.

Children became restless and ran between the quilts. The trill of little girls giggling filled the air. A pair of boys ran by, hitting a three-foot wooden hoop with sticks to keep it rolling. A dog nipped at their heels.

When Troy finished eating, one piece of chicken, a biscuit, and Liv's portion of the cake remained. He packed the empty dishes and leftovers back into the box. "Everything was delicious. Thank you."

"You're welcome."

He scooted closer. When she shifted to move away, he reached across her and planted his hand on the quilt. He spoke softly into her ear. "I know you're afraid I'll hurt you again. I won't. I promise."

The episode with Violet last year hadn't been his fault. She had caught him off guard. And before he could disentangle himself from her, Liv had seen and then run off.

But Violet wasn't the first gal Liv had caught him with in a compromising position. Was it his fault women were attracted to him? It wasn't like he asked any of them to throw themselves at him. But Liv still blamed *him* for *their* actions.

He studied her profile. Her perfectly straight nose. Her full rosy lips. Her corn silk hair with wisps of curls around her face. He could tell he had weakened her resolve today. "Liv."

She turned her face to him.

He caressed her cheek. "I love you." He saw pleasure fill her eyes. He knew it. For all her bluster and refusal, she still loved him.

He continued to caress her cheek. When she didn't slap his hand away, he knew he'd broken through her resistance. He leaned forward. He would kiss her, and she would melt into his arms like she used to. It couldn't be a long kiss in this crowd, but it didn't need to be. He felt her breath on his lips.

Something smacked the side of his head, and the offending wooden hoop flopped over on his lap. The two boys with sticks and the scruffy brown mutt romped onto their quilt.

Liv turned away. The wall shutting him out went back up. She petted the dog.

They had spoiled his moment.

Troy flopped back, staring up at a sky the color of Liv's eyes. He'd escorted her to the event, *not* peeked at her box when he'd wanted to, been her partner in the three-legged race, taken her on the hayride, and won her box. And now all his work today was for naught. Defeated by a pair of eight-year-old boys.

"Sorry, Mr. Morrison."

Troy waved a hand at the boys from where he lay. "Not a problem."

The kids ran off, rolling the hoop with the sticks. *Tap, tap, tap.*

Liv's shoulders quivered.

Was she laughing?

Finding humor in this could be good.

Maybe he could regain the moment. He sat back up and laced his fingers with hers.

She bit her lower lip, not quite hiding a smile.

With a finger under her chin, he turned her to face him again.

Someone cleared his throat.

Troy glanced up sideways.

Anita and George stood beside their quilt.

He willed them away, but Anita spoke. "They're going to start the bonfire competitions soon. Want to come?"

Nick and Felicity joined them. "Do come."

Troy squeezed Liv's hand to keep her in place. To no avail.

"I'd love to." Liv pushed to her feet, rather awkwardly with him still holding her hand. She gazed down at him, her eyes twinkling. "Are you going to join us?"

She knew very well he wanted to stay right where he was with her at his side.

Nick and George gave him apologetic shrugs.

Liv's mouth turned up in a sly smile. "You don't want George or Nick to win the log-throwing contests, do you?"

Since she was going, he might as well, too. He tightened his grip on her hand and heaved himself up, mostly using his legs. Still, his hold on her almost pulled her down. He gladly would have caught her—maybe he should have tried harder.

Reluctantly, he released her hand to grab the box and quilt. After joining the others heading down Spring Street to Front Street, Troy walked with Nick and George behind the ladies.

"Sorry we interrupted you and Olivia," George said. "Anita wanted to go to the bonfire. Her folks wouldn't let her unless the two of you and your girls went."

"Not a problem. We would have ended up down at the beach anyway." The bonfire, reserved for the young couples, was where Troy would get his kiss. Two contests, one of speed and the other of strength. Men could enter one or the other. The winners could steal a kiss from their gals.

Several huge piles of chopped wood waited on the beach for spectators. The central pile, already built and doused with kerosene, stood five feet wide by five feet high, the base the rest of the wood would be built upon. Ten piles surrounded this, five of cordwood and five of large heavy pieces.

Troy set the box and quilt down and rubbed his hands together. "So which do you want me to enter?"

Liv shrugged. "I don't think you will win either, so it doesn't really matter."

He took her teasing as a challenge. She probably hoped he wouldn't win. But he would.

Nick slapped him on the back. "I'm entering the speed competition."

George nodded. "Me, too."

Troy clasped them both on the shoulders. "I wouldn't want to make the two of you look bad in front of your girls, so I'll enter the strength contest." It was the harder of the two.

His friends seemed pleased he wouldn't be competing against them. Not that they would admit it. But only one of them could win.

First, the speed competition. Five men each started with an equal pile of wood. The first one to get all his wood into the bonfire won. Those who wanted to compete drew straws to see who the five lucky men would be. Each participant must throw his wood to the middle of the fire one at a time. If any rolled off, he had to retoss it, even if it was aflame.

George drew the shortest. Disappointed, he stepped back.

Anita stood only a couple of inches shorter than George. "Consolation prize." She kissed him. George locked his arms around her and kissed her back.

Liv sucked in a breath and moved to rescue Anita, but Troy hooked his arm around her waist. "Leave them be."

"But—"

"Leave them be, or I'll do the same to you right now."

She stomped one little foot and stiffened. "Why are you so exasperating?"

"Just part of my charming personality." She was cute when he flustered her.

Nick drew one of the long straws.

Each of the five chosen stood twenty yards up the beach. At the signal, they would run. The fastest runner got the closest pile and the advantage.

A man threw a burning log up into the air. When it hit the middle of the pile, the runners took off. The kerosene-soaked wood caught fire in a *whoosh*.

Nick reached the piles second.

Not bad.

But he kept dropping the wood and not throwing the logs high enough onto the heap. He came in third.

The first-place winner grabbed his girl and gave her a long kiss to the hoots of the crowd.

Though Nick returned in defeat, Felicity said, "Congratulations."

"What for? I lost."

"You're the only one I saw finish."

He got her meaning and kissed her.

That was often how it went. Even those who didn't win received kisses.

But Troy wouldn't likely be so fortunate. Liv was too stubborn. Unless he won, he wouldn't be getting a kiss. And he was determined not to be left out.

Each man would take his turn tossing the bigger logs up onto the pile that now stood higher and burned hotter. If the log didn't stay up on top, the participant was eliminated.

Troy removed his vest and cap and handed them to Liv. "Hold these for me." Rolling up his sleeves, he took his place.

Each man succeeded in rounds one and two. One was eliminated in round three, two in round four. The hunks of wood grew progressively bigger and heavier.

The competition came down to Troy and Albert. He knew the blacksmith would be a tough competitor.

Troy wiped sweat from his forehead, hefted a log with both hands and took several deep breaths before he swung it up and let go.

The log landed on the top but near the edge. Everyone cheered and then caught their breaths as it dislodged another log and tumbled back down. The crowd expressed their disappointment in a collective "Ooh!"

When it rolled near him, he jumped out of the path.

He wasn't out yet. If Albert missed, they would still be tied and have another go.

As Albert heaved his piece of wood, Troy held his breath. It hit near the top and tumbled back.

Troy hoisted the log the next size bigger. If he didn't make this one, he doubted he could succeed with the next larger.

He glanced back at Liv's unworried expression. She didn't think he'd make it. He'd show her. If the Scots could throw cabers the size of full-grown trees, he could do this. He drew in a deep breath, held it a moment before exhaling and heaved.

The crowd cheered when it landed solidly on the top.

He hoped his opponent wouldn't be as successful.

As Albert readied to release his log, his foot slipped on the pebbly beach. His attempt crashed into the side of the bonfire.

Troy threw up his arms in victory and strode toward Liv.

Her eyes widened. She held up her finger and stepped back. "No. You are all sweaty."

He crooked his finger toward her.

She shook her head and stepped back again.

Nick and George moved in behind her to stop her retreat.

She glanced back at them, knowing she was trapped. She let her shoulders droop in defeat. "Very well."

He knew she expected him to just kiss her and be done with it. But if he was going to get only one kiss this day, he'd make it count. He dipped her, forcing her to hold on to him.

She gasped.

He placed a gentle, lingering kiss on her lips. And she

responded, kissing him back. Though he ended the kiss, he didn't set her upright. "That wasn't so bad, was it?"

Her eyelids fluttered open. "What?"

He chuckled and righted her.

Liv's straw sailor hat sat askew on her head. He straightened it for her and tapped the top of it.

The day was going well, indeed.

With the sun dipping below the horizon, the temperature dropped. Troy took the quilt and wrapped it around himself.

Liv put her hands on her hips. "I believe that's mine."

He opened it up. "I'll share."

Couples bundled themselves together and sat around the fire.

He doubted Liv would concede. So he fixed the problem by wrapping his arm around her and sitting her down with him.

They faced the water, and she gasped as the first fireworks exploded over the harbor.

That was how he felt when he kissed Liv. Lights and color bursting inside him. He just wanted to sit here with her. Once the fireworks had ended, he knew he needed to walk her home. But he didn't need to release her from the quilt.

He stood, lifting her to her feet. She leaned against him.

Nick handed him his box, and he tucked it under his free arm while maintaining a hold on the quilt.

Liv didn't protest or say anything on the way to her house.

Once they arrived in her yard, he faced her and kept his arm around her. He bent forward and kissed her. Her lips were soft, warm and yielding. "So have you forgiven me?"

With a smile, she ducked out of his grasp and pulled the quilt off him. "Perhaps tomorrow." She rolled the quilt around her arms.

He'd come to hate those two words. "I'll hold you to that."

She lightly ran up the steps of her porch and turned. "You do that, Mr. Morrison. You do that." She blew him a kiss and slipped inside.

His jaw slackened. Was she saying tomorrow? All this nonsense would be over tomorrow? She would forgive him? Not that this little game of theirs hadn't been fun, but he would be glad to be done with it.

He turned on one foot and whistled his way home.

Chapter 3

Olivia woke to rain tapping on the roof. She didn't care. This was going to be a glorious day in spite of the weather. She stretched her arms above her head and smiled. The rain made the air smell fresh and new. Just like the day.

Troy had gone a whole year without one mishap with another woman. At least that she knew of. And she didn't want to think otherwise. She could trust him now and therefore forgive him.

She hastened to put on her prettiest pink dress and then prepared breakfast for Mother and Gran.

Mother patted the table from where she sat in her wheelchair. "Sit and eat."

"I ate enough while I was cooking."

Gran gave a toothy grin. "Have you and that handsome boy finally reconciled?"

"Today."

Mother smiled, as well. "With the look on your face when you came home, I figured you two made up last night."

"It's about time." Gran eyed Olivia. "Yesterday was a final test for him, wasn't it?"

"I was never testing him. But I needed to learn to trust him again."

"And now you have?" Gran asked.

"Oh, yes. He was so sweet yesterday. And attentive." She ignored the fact that he'd smiled at Violet. That girl needed to understand that Troy was her beau and she'd best find her own. Violet thought her family's wealth entitled her to anything—or anyone—she wanted.

"I'm glad," Mother said. "We'll see you later. Have a nice time."

"Oh, I will." Olivia kissed her mother on the cheek and then Gran.

From the stand by the door, she grabbed the blue umbrella Troy had given her. She didn't care that it didn't match her dress. This whole past year she had avoided using it. Wielding the pretty blue gift might have given Troy the idea she'd forgiven him. But now that she had, she was happy to use it for protection.

She wrapped herself in a shawl as she stepped outside and pushed open the umbrella. She fingered the white lace that lined the inside. The only one like it in town.

She would need to be vigilant to keep her dress from being ruined by mud. She wanted to look nice for Troy.

Troy sat behind his desk in his office at the bank and couldn't help but smile. Liv had all but said last night that she would officially forgive him today. Unofficially, he knew she already had. He couldn't wait for his workday to be over so he could see her. He would gaze into her sky-blue eyes, ask one final time for forgiveness and kiss her.

From his vest pocket, he pulled out a small black velvet pouch, loosened the strings, and poured the contents onto his palm. Set in a white-gold band, a solitaire blue zircon sparkled. It was the sapphire's paler cousin and the color of Liv's eyes.

Jack, the office boy, poked his head through Troy's doorway. "Mr. Jones wants you."

"Thank you." He returned the ring to the pouch and pocketed it. He had bought it six months ago, but he'd known he would have to wait until just the right time for Liv to accept it. Tonight was that night.

Troy stepped into the bank manager's office as requested. He stopped short at the sight of the man's wife and daughter. "I can come back later."

Mr. Jones waved him in. "Come in. This concerns you."

A sudden unsettled feeling twisted in the pit of his stomach. He took one more step inside but left the door open. He smiled at Mrs. Jones seated in a chair and at Violet standing next to her. Then he turned back to his boss. "You wanted to see me, sir?"

"What plans do you have for this coming Saturday?"

That was four days away. Other than seeing Liv? None. Not that she knew about it yet. He planned to see her tonight and every day and night for the rest of his life.

"No plans?" The bank manager's mouth spread into a wide smile. "Good."

Troy regretted not speaking up faster but didn't quite know why.

"My wife has arranged a dinner party for Saturday."

No.

"It appears we are one guest short."

Don't say it.

"You will be Violet's escort."

Noooo. "That's very kind of you, but I must decline."

His boss pulled his eyebrows low. "I thought you had no plans. I've seen the way you look at my daughter."

He looked at all the ladies the same. Except Liv. She was different.

Violet's mouth twisted into a possessive smile. She sashayed close to him and hooked her arm through his.

He wanted to jerk away from her, but it would not bode well for him if he rejected his boss's daughter. Why couldn't he have said he had a previous engagement? Trapped, he swallowed hard. "I would be honored, sir." He nearly choked on his answer.

Violet tilted her head onto his shoulder.

Troy stiffened. This was not good. Not good at all. He had to figure some way out of this without offending his boss and losing his job.

And without Liv finding out.

Olivia couldn't believe the scene before her eyes. Troy with Violet snuggled up to him.

Images of her father kissing Widow Baxter crashed over her like a violent storm. She'd successfully pushed the memory away and bought into his fictitious death. Lived the lie so long, she believed it. Until seeing Troy with Violet again brought it all hurling back. The pain of abandonment. The humility of betrayal. She had pushed the memories and pain aside before. She could do it again.

She had wanted Troy to be different. But he wasn't.

He just stood there talking with his boss with Violet securely at his side. He evidently wanted Mr. Jones to think there was something between him and Violet. He was probably trying to win favors with his boss.

Olivia couldn't watch any more. She raced out of the bank and ran into a gentleman on the boardwalk.

He gripped her shoulders to keep them both from tumbling into the muddy street. "Pardon me, miss."

"I'm sorry." She turned away from him and dashed out into the rain, not bothering to dodge puddles. Not caring if her dress got dirty. Rain soaked through all her layers of clothing right to her skin. Her skirt hung heavy with rain and dragged in the mud.

Breathing hard, she knocked with a clenched fist on the Devlins' door.

Missy, the youngest Devlin, opened the door and gasped. "What happened to you?"

Olivia must look bedraggled. She pushed a wet tendril from her face. "Forgot my umbrella. Is Felicity here?" Her lips quivered.

Mrs. Devlin appeared behind the girl. "You poor child. Come in out of the wet and cold. Missy, go get your sister." She touched Olivia's arm. "Come into the kitchen and warm yourself by the stove."

Olivia sat in the straight-back chair Mrs. Devlin pulled up to the stove. "Thank you."

"I'll get you a towel to dry your hair." Mrs. Devlin scurried out.

Taking a deep breath, Olivia spread the folds of her skirt out so it would dry quicker. The bottom four inches were spattered with mud.

Felicity burst into the kitchen with a towel and handed it to Olivia. "What happened? Is it your mother? Granny?"

Olivia felt the tears burn her eyes. No, she would not

cry. Never again would she cry over that man. But the tears came anyway. "I *hate* him."

Felicity pulled up a chair. "But you were getting on so well yesterday."

Nice how Felicity didn't even have to ask of whom she spoke. "Apparently not as well as I thought."

"What happened? Did something happen when he walked you home last night? Did he do something unspeakable?"

Oh, no. He had played at being the perfect gentleman. Making her believe all was well between them. Making her believe he was faithful to her. Making her believe he loved only her. "He was with *her*."

"Her who? When?"

"Violet. This morning." Olivia tried to push the image from her mind, only to have it replaced by the image of him kissing Violet a year ago. He'd promised!

"No." Felicity shook her head. "He's devoted to you."

"Evidently not. He prefers her dark hair and exotic look to my pale, washed-out one." She put her hands on her cheeks.

"No. You're beautiful. He doesn't love you for how you look. What was he doing with her?"

"She was at the bank with him."

"Now, don't jump to conclusions. Her father does run the bank. It's perfectly natural for her to be there."

Olivia moved her hands in tight, frustrated circles. "She was hanging on his arm. Then she put her head on his shoulder." She whimpered.

After a moment, her friend said, "What did Troy do? Push her away? Tell me he pushed her away. You stayed this time to see his reaction, didn't you?"

"He did nothing. He stood there with her wrapped around his arm and did *absolutely* nothing."

Felicity touched her arm. "Livia, breathe."

"I don't ever want to again." Unfortunately, she had no choice and inhaled. "Do you think he's been seeing her this whole time?"

"Certainly not. We would have known. I'm sure he has an explanation."

"He always does." Just like her father. She slapped away the tears on her cheeks. "I guess that's it. After dallying around for six years, it's finally over." Why couldn't he have just asked her to marry him back then? Instead he had to go to college and *prove* himself to her father. Then Father had passed away. At least that was what they'd told everyone to avoid the humiliation of his abandoning them for another woman. And then last year was the Violet incident. Troy's worst yet.

Felicity hugged her. "I'm so sorry."

She was, too. She would never marry now. For she could never love anyone else as she loved him. And he couldn't be trusted.

Troy bounded up the Bradshaws' steps in one leap and knocked. He'd had a difficult time waiting all day to see Liv. He'd hoped she would have stopped by to see him. But he was the man and should be doing the calling on her.

Granny Bradshaw opened the door and smiled. "Good to see you. Come in."

As he stepped over the threshold, he patted his vest pocket. Tonight would be the beginning of their future.

Mrs. Bradshaw wheeled over in her chair. "Good evening, Troy. Go on into the parlor. I'll send Olivia in."

Granny Bradshaw added, "And we'll leave the two of you alone."

He appreciated that. He sat on the settee and then

stood. Walked over to the hearth and back to the settee. Too restless to sit, he returned to the hearth. He would look good standing there. And he could easily see Liv when she came in.

Liv entered with a tray of tea and chocolate cake. She wore a striking blue dress with black pinstripes. She had apparently dressed up for him, but she wasn't smiling.

He'd expected her to be smiling. Was something wrong? Troy wasn't used to being rattled. He took a deep breath and pushed the disquiet aside. "Hello, Liv." He reached for his vest pocket.

Her expression remained neutral as she set the tray down on the serving table. She sat on the edge of the wingback chair facing the settee and looked up at him. "Cake?"

He left the velvet bag where it was and took the offered plate. He sat on the settee by himself but left ample room for her. He patted the seat. "Sit beside me?"

She handed him a cup of tea. Taking neither cake nor tea, she shifted back in the chair. "I'm comfortable here."

Why was Liv acting so strange?

"Is everything all right?"

She smoothed a nonexistent wrinkle in her skirt. "I don't know. Is it?"

He put his cup and plate back on the tray. "Apparently not. Tell me what's bothering you."

"Very well." She folded her hands in her lap and raised her blue gaze to him. "I sense that there's something you need to tell me."

The hair on the back of his neck prickled. "Like what?"

Olivia stood, crossed to the hearth, and swiveled to face him. "Think, Troy. Think real hard."

A sudden sour taste in his mouth caused the back of

his throat to ache. Did she know? She couldn't possibly. Someone must have told her. But who? "Who told you?"

She narrowed her eyes. "Told me what?"

She wanted him to say it, to admit it. But he could tell that she knew. Maybe it was Violet herself who'd made sure Liv knew.

His chest tightened, and he couldn't draw in a full breath. He held his hands out, palms up. "I don't want to go to this supper."

Her eyes widened in anger. "Supper? You're taking *her* to supper?"

Wasn't that what she was hinting at? She obviously knew some of it, so he might as well come clean.

"Violet's parents are throwing a dinner party, and I'm to be her escort. I don't have a choice. Isn't that what you're talking about? Someone told you I was going to be at their supper party on Saturday with Violet?"

"No one told me anything. I saw her wrapped around your arm with my own eyes."

She had seen? She had been there? His heart constricted. She always managed to catch him in unfortunate situations. And today was going to be the day she forgave him and put all this nonsense behind them. Why did she have to see?

He stood, holding out his hands. "Liv, that's not my fault. She—"

"That's the problem. Nothing is ever your fault. Poor Troy, everyone takes advantage of him."

"I couldn't push her away with my boss there." He reached for her hand.

She jerked away from him. "Don't touch me." She turned to leave.

He couldn't let her. He grabbed her upper arms and made her face him. "Let me explain."

She wrestled to free herself but gave up quickly and hit her fists on his chest. "You promised! You promised!"

"I know. But there is nothing between Violet and me. You know that."

She kept thumping her fists against him. "Then you should have pushed her away. You should have. Let me go."

"Not until you calm down." He wrapped his arms around her and held her close to keep her from hurting herself.

She struggled in his embrace for only a moment and then went stiff. "Let. Me. Go."

He sensed if he did, he might never have her in his arms again. With a deep sigh, he released her. "If I rejected Violet right there in front of my boss, I would have been fired."

She stepped back. "So Violet and your job mean more to you than me?"

"No. But I can't take care of you if I don't have work."

Olivia stared at him vacantly.

Didn't she believe him? "Liv, I love *you*."

She shook her head. "I can't put up with this anymore. I can't always be wondering if you are with her or some other girl."

"I've never been with another girl. Only you. You are the only one I care about."

"You have allowed yourself to get into this position. You haven't gained any wisdom. I want you to leave."

"Please, Liv. We can talk about this."

"I just can't." Her blue eyes brimmed with unshed tears. "If you won't leave, then I will." She strode out of the parlor and to her room across the hall. She closed the door almost silently.

But she might as well have slammed it for the impact it had on him. She had shut him out as though she'd never cared.

Her mother and grandmother stood in the hallway. They both had sympathetic expressions for him.

"She'll settle down in a day or two," Granny Bradshaw said. "I'm sure she will."

That was a nice sentiment, but he doubted it. Liv's temper had a long memory.

Liv peered through the crack between the curtains and watched Troy walk down the path and turn onto the street. A part of her wanted to call him back and forgive him. But the part of her that was tired of being hurt by him wouldn't let her. She pressed her palm to the cold glass.

A lone tear trickled down her cheek.

Chapter 4

When Troy arrived at work the next morning and opened the bank, he noticed a lone umbrella in the stand. Blue lined with white lace. He removed it from the brass container. Liv *had* been here. And left in a hurry. She had accused him of not pushing Violet away, so she had evidently stayed long enough to notice that.

His heart hoped she would get over this soon enough and forgive him. His head said otherwise.

He took the umbrella to his office. He didn't want anyone else to accidentally take it home. Having it near made Liv seem closer somehow. Somehow he had to make her understand. He didn't want to lose her and knew he needed to *do* something.

He waited until his boss had been in his office for a while, then went to see him. He hadn't wanted to go too soon and seem overly eager. He knocked on the closed door.

"Enter," Mr. Jones called.

Troy took a deep breath and turned the knob. "Do you have a minute?"

His boss looked up from where he sat. "Of course."

Troy closed the door and crossed to the desk.

Mr. Jones frowned. "You look tired."

Troy had spent half the night going over the events of the day and what he should have done and said. And he prayed for a quick resolution to his dinner party problem. And that Liv would understand and not be angry with him for another year. "About the supper on Saturday." He could speak man-to-man without hurting Violet's feelings.

Mr. Jones gave a Cheshire cat smile. "I can't tell you how happy you have made my wife and daughter."

That was not what Troy wanted to hear.

His boss went on. "Some fuss about having an odd number of guests at the table."

"Sir, I was wondering if we could find someone else in my stead."

"I can't believe a young man in your position would turn down a free meal."

Troy's position was not destitution but rather love. This "free" meal put him at a terrible disadvantage with Liv and could cost him dearly. He took a deep breath and forged ahead. "Your daughter is quite beautiful, but I don't...well, *care* for Violet in the way you suggested yesterday. It might be best to have someone else be her escort."

His boss's smile faded, and he leaned forward. "My daughter wants you, and you *will* be there. Understood?"

He did. "But why me? Certainly there are other eligible men who would be suitable." And willing. "What about Titus Berg? Or William Ecker? Or—"

Mr. Jones held up his hand. "All worthy suggestions,

but my daughter asked for you." He turned his palms up. "We are only mere men. How are we to understand the workings of the female mind? It's just a supper, boy, not a marriage proposal."

He hoped Violet understood that. Dare he argue further? Or flat-out refuse?

"Anything else?"

Losing his job would serve no purpose. Liv would still be angry with him. It would accomplish nothing. The damage was already done in Liv's eyes. No turning back. "No, sir."

"Then I suggest you get back to your duties."

Troy returned to his office. Since it was Violet who requested his presence, she was the key in this. Maybe he could convince her to change her mind. He would reason with her.

Meeting with her would be risky, especially if Liv found out. But well worth it if he got out of the supper party.

Olivia woke to knocking. Her swollen eyes wouldn't open.

"Olivia?"

She forced her puffy lids up and squinted. The room was too bright. "Uh." She blinked to clear her vision.

The knob rattled, and the door opened. Gran stepped in. "We were wondering if you're feeling all right."

"Of course I am." Olivia's mouth watered at the scent of cooked bacon.

"You don't usually sleep this late."

"What time is it?" She sat up and yawned.

"Nine o'clock."

No wonder it was so bright. She was always up by six or six-thirty. Last night she had been too upset to sleep and had cried silently for hours. "I'm sorry for oversleeping. You made breakfast?"

"Your mother and I did."

"You two shouldn't have had to do that." In the five years since Mother's accident, Olivia always cooked breakfast.

"Don't worry about it. Your mother and I are capable of cooking a meal."

"I'll get dressed and be right out."

Gran closed the door behind her.

Olivia threw back the covers and put her bare feet on the scratchy wool rug beside her bed. She dressed quickly, brushed out her braid, and twisted her hair onto the back of her head, shoving pins into it as she headed for her door.

When she entered the parlor, Gran and Mother looked up from their handwork. One sewing. The other knitting. Mother spoke. "Are you all right? You're not catching something, are you?"

She'd caught something all right. Troy with Violet. Again. "I'm fine."

"There's a plate in the warmer for you. Bring it in here to eat so you don't have to sit alone. Coffee's in the pot on the stove."

Olivia continued into the kitchen. With a towel, she pulled the plate out of the warming oven. The bacon was crisp the way she liked it, but the eggs and the biscuit looked dry. She poured a cup of coffee and returned to the parlor. She preferred tea but didn't have the energy to make any.

She sat and ate. Well, mostly just poked at her food and sipped her coffee.

Mother rested her hands in her lap with the quilt block she was piecing together. "You look tired, dear."

Olivia could try to deny her fatigue, but what good would that do? Mother would know. She already did. "I didn't sleep well."

Gran finished a row of knitting, flipped the sleeve around and continued. "It's no wonder with the row you had with Troy last night."

The click, click, clicking of her needles might as well have been the clicking of her tongue in disapproval. She always did fancy Troy. She didn't know him the way Olivia did.

"Don't hang on to disappointments." Mother picked up her sewing again. "There are too many real tragedies to dwell on minor indiscretions."

"It wasn't minor. He was with another woman." Just like her father.

"But wasn't it Violet? You know he doesn't care for her."

"Then he should have pushed her away. Mother, I would think you of all people would understand. Troy is just like Father."

"Your father was a good man. He just couldn't cope after my accident. I don't blame him for leaving."

"You should." Oh, Mother would never speak ill of Father. "I can't put up with Troy's behavior any longer." This was how life with Troy would be. Always wondering. "I'm done with him."

"I doubt that." Mother voiced what Olivia's heart told her.

Doubt or not, she had to make it so. She would avoid Troy until her heart learned to obey.

Troy lifted the ornate brass knocker and tapped it twice. The vibration resonated up his arm and sent a foreboding shudder through him. Maybe he should leave.

A maid opened the door. "May I help you, sir?"

He wanted to say no. He wanted to leave. He took a deep breath. "I'm here to see Miss Violet Jones."

"Very good, sir. Right this way." She showed him into a lavishly decorated parlor. "Whom shall I say is calling?"

"Troy Morrison." He had never been in his boss's home before. He much preferred the Bradshaws' welcoming, simpler parlor. He pulled at his collar. Like a mouse who had willingly entered a trap, he waited for the cat to arrive.

He looked around. A large mantel clock of carved dark wood sat above the fireplace. A smaller crystal clock on a tabletop. And a third brass-framed clock on a secretary desk. An empty china vase on the mantel. A pair of porcelain figurines of a boy and a girl. Polished rocks in a brass bowl. A carved wooden box too small to be functional. Queen Anne–style furniture set on a lush red-and-blue carpet. He shook his head at all the impractical trinkets.

According to all three clocks, nearly fifteen minutes had passed. Where was Violet?

"Mr. Morrison." The syrupy voice came from behind him. "I never expected you to call on me."

Troy spun around. The cat had arrived. He swallowed hard. If he dealt with Violet carefully, he could get out of the supper party and still keep his job.

Violet wore a costly jade-green gown. She crossed to the settee and lowered herself but didn't look as though she was actually touching the seat. How could she manage to appear to hover like that? She motioned next to her. "Please, have a seat."

Using Liv's trick, he sat in a chair across from her. "I wanted to speak to you about the dinner party."

"Not from over there. Sit here." She touched the seat next to her.

"I don't think that's such a good idea."

"If you wish to speak with me, then I insist." The cat had issued her demand.

He didn't move.

She rose. "Good day, Mr. Morrison." A dismissal.

He shot to his feet. "Very well."

She smiled triumphantly and lowered herself back down, hovering.

Coming had been a bad idea. Violet enjoyed the power she wielded over him. He sat as close to the end and as far away from her as he could. She didn't seem to mind.

He gritted his teeth and forced the words out. "About supper on Saturday."

She folded her hands and rested them on her lap. "I'm expecting a grand time with you."

Not likely. He curled his hands into fists. "Why do you want *me* there?"

"Why not?"

Because he didn't belong there. "You know I'm in love with Olivia."

"You are too good for her."

No. It was the other way around. He was a simple miner's son. Olivia's father had been a businessman.

"Has she even forgiven you for us being together last year?"

"We were never together."

"We kissed. I would call that together."

"You kissed me."

She shrugged as though it were a detail too minor to comment on. "Has she forgiven you?"

"She had until yesterday."

Violet's mouth twisted into a smile. "The look on her face was exhilarating."

"You saw her at the bank?" That must have been the reason Violet had behaved so openly. Only nineteen and already cunning. "Why don't you like Olivia?"

"I really don't care one whit about her. But she has had you wrapped around her finger for far too long. No other girl stood a chance at winning your heart. Maybe now you'll see that there are plenty of other girls more than willing to be Mrs. Troy Morrison. I've done you a favor."

No, she hadn't. Troy held his breath as Mr. Jones's words came back to him. *It's not a marriage proposal.* He was in quite a spot with Violet. One wrong word, and she could get her father to fire him for no reason. He let the air seep out of his lungs. "Why me? You could have just about any other man in town."

She waved a delicate hand in the air. "Oh, none of those silly boys interest me. You are the only one I've not been able to attract. I'll venture to guess that you didn't even notice I was gone for *five* months."

She had been gone? He couldn't admit that he hadn't paid attention to that. He recalled his boss mentioning something about it. Was Violet doing this because he hadn't said anything about her absence?

"Why would you want a man who doesn't love you? Don't you want love?"

"I suppose love would be nice, but I'd rather be the envy of every woman in town."

She made it sound so simple, but what an empty, sad life. He saw no way of talking himself out of this with her. If anything, he'd made matters worse.

Nausea rolled in the pit of his stomach. He stood. "I have to get back to work."

Violet rose and blocked his path. "You *will* be here Saturday."

He gritted his teeth again. "I don't see where I have much choice."

"No." She smiled, seeming to enjoy his torture. "You don't."

He hurried out the door, down the walk, and through the gate. He looked up in time to see Felicity Devlin staring at him from across the street. *Great. Just great.* Almost as bad as Liv herself catching him exiting Violet's house.

Felicity shook her head and planted her fists on her hips as though she expected him to give an account for himself.

That might not be bad.

He crossed the street to her. "It's not what you think."

"Isn't it?"

"No."

She widened her eyes in question. "Then explain yourself."

Liv was usually content to jump to her own conclusions. Being given the chance to explain himself right off was different.

"My boss has insisted that I attend a supper at his house on Saturday."

"I know."

So she had spoken to Liv already. "I don't want to go."

"I find that hard to believe when you have run off in the middle of the day to visit the lady you will be keeping company with."

He glanced back at the house. "I wasn't visiting her—I mean, I did go there to talk to her." He stopped and took a deep breath. "Apparently, it was Violet's idea to have me as a supper guest."

"Don't you mean *her* companion?"

He didn't want the conversation to get capsized by the details. "Look. I don't even want to go. Mr. Jones is insisting. If I don't attend, I'll lose my job. I went to talk Violet out of having me there."

"How did that go over?"

"Not well. I think I made matters worse."

She folded her arms. "So what are you going to do about it?"

He held out his hands. "There is nothing I can do. I'm trapped. You believe me, don't you?"

"Perhaps."

He became cognizant of where Felicity stood in relation to her house and Liv's. A sinking feeling washed over him. "You're on your way to Liv's, aren't you?"

She nodded. "She was thoroughly upset yesterday. I want to make sure she's all right."

He was painfully aware of Liv's ire. "Are you going to tell her about this?" *Please say no.*

"I haven't decided."

Relief mixed with his dread. He couldn't believe she might keep it to herself. "Please don't tell her. I'm trying my best to fix this. If Liv finds out I was here, it will only make her more upset unnecessarily. You wouldn't want that now, would you?"

She shook her finger at him and narrowed her eyes. "Don't you try to sweet-talk me. I'll think about it, only because you are Nick's best friend. But you better not be seen with her again."

"Thank you. I'm not planning on it. And I will think of some way to get out of this supper."

"You had better."

Now he just needed to wiggle out of supper. But how—and still keep his job?

* * *

Olivia walked down Spring Street with Felicity. She had been pleasantly surprised by her best friend's visit. Felicity had insisted Olivia go with her, wanting her to help choose yarn for a shawl she was going to knit for her mother's birthday in the fall. Olivia knew her friend didn't need her help. Felicity was on a mission to cheer Olivia up.

She doubted anything could lift her spirits. She needed to sort through her feelings for Troy, both the painful ones as well as the good ones. Then to decide if she loved him enough to put up with the hurtful things about him, or if her father's betrayal and faithlessness had rendered her incapable of trusting.

Stepping up onto the boardwalk in front of the mercantile, she noticed a well-dressed man standing across the street. Wasn't that the same man she'd run into outside the bank yesterday? She couldn't quite tell.

Felicity opened the door for Olivia. "I think you're being followed."

"You've seen him, too?" She glanced at Felicity and back to the man, who had turned and was walking up the street. She stepped inside. "Why do you think he's following me and not you?"

"I saw him walking down your street when I arrived." Felicity closed the door and peeked out the window. "Have you ever seen him before?"

"I think I saw him outside the bank yesterday." She'd run into him, and he'd kept her from tumbling into the muddy street.

"Who is he?"

"I don't know." This was preposterous. Just because she had seen this stranger in the past couple of days didn't mean he was following her. "I think it's just coincidence that we have both seen him. Friday Harbor isn't so big that someone new in town wouldn't be seen over and over." She glanced out the window. "He's gone. If he were truly following me, wouldn't he still be there?"

"I suppose."

"Nothing more than happenstance." Olivia walked over to the flat bin of yarn. "What color are you thinking of?"

Felicity picked up a skein. "This red would be pretty on her." She picked up another skein. "Or what about this royal blue?"

Violet sauntered up to the bin, fingered some white yarn, and then gave a smug smile. "Troy is coming to my house on Saturday for supper."

Olivia took a controlling breath. She would like to scratch Violet's eyes out. But maybe she should let Violet have Troy and be done with him. No. Anyone but Violet. "I know."

"He's going to be *my* partner."

Olivia refused to be baited. "So?"

"So…it appears the better woman—me—has won."

Felicity squared her shoulders. "I don't know that *better* is the right word. I would use conniving, wily, manipulative. Troy loves Olivia, so declaring yourself the winner is a bit ill-considered."

Olivia appreciated her friend standing up for her. She wasn't up for verbal sparring with Violet.

"Call me what you like, but I have the best catch in town." Violet turned with a swish and sashayed away.

Felicity patted Olivia's arm. "Don't worry. Troy would never choose her over you."

How could she be so sure? Troy was attending a formal supper at Violet's house.

When they left the mercantile with the red yarn, the man in the fine suit was nowhere to be seen.

After supper, Olivia poured hot water from the teakettle into her dishwater. She dipped her finger in to test the temperature and jerked it back out. She would need to wait a few minutes before plunging her hands in.

"Olivia, dear?" Mother called from the parlor. "Would you come in here?"

She wiped her hands on a towel and walked into the other room. "Would you like some more tea?"

Mother glanced at her cup. "No, I'm fine." She opened her mouth to say something else but stopped at a knock on the door.

"I'll get that. I'll be right back."

"Thank you, dear."

She opened the door.

Troy.

She swung the door shut.

"Olivia Bradshaw!" Mother scolded. "You open that door right this instance." Mother had obviously known he was approaching and had called Olivia into the parlor so she would be the one to answer his knock. Mother and Gran hadn't accepted that her courtship with Troy was over. In time they would. Just as her heart would.

Taking a deep breath and schooling her heart to not react, Olivia opened the door. Success.

Troy stood on the porch with her umbrella in hand. He held it out. "You forgot this at the bank." Then he smiled.

Her heart danced. *Traitor.* She struggled to regain control and then said, "You may keep it. I won't have need of it."

Though his dimpled smile remained steadfast on his lips, it left his eyes. He reached around the door frame and slipped the umbrella into the stand. "Maybe you'll have use for it later."

She would rather drown in a downpour than have him see her using a gift from him. But she was glad to have her umbrella back where it belonged. If she didn't stop all this back and forth, she would be swooning into his arms by the week's end.

"Liv, I'm doing everything I can to get out of this supper."

She hoped he succeeded. "Don't trouble yourself on my account."

"I know you don't mean that."

She didn't and could feel herself weakening, so she straightened her shoulders. Once he'd gotten out of the meal, she would reconsider. But not before. If he didn't leave soon, she would cave.

Gran spoke from behind her. "Troy, would you like to come in?"

Troy's smile brightened. "That's a very kind invitation." He glanced at Olivia. "But I must decline. I have some business to attend to."

Olivia understood the look in his eyes. He was going to work on getting out of the supper two nights hence.

He dipped his head, turned, and left.

She appreciated his not pushing her. She watched him go and slowly closed the door.

As she walked through the parlor on her way to the kitchen, Mother spoke. "Come sit down, dear."

"I have the dishwater ready."

"It'll keep. Sit." Mother's voice was soft and resigned.

Olivia sensed something was wrong and sat on the settee next to her. "Are you feeling all right?"

Mother patted her hand. "Yes, I'm fine. It's about your father."

What about Father? He wasn't coming back, was he? Did she want him to? Not after what he'd done. And they had told everyone he'd died. His return would be salt in wounds that refused to heal.

"We waited until after you had your fun at the Independence celebrations, but it shouldn't be put off any longer."

Olivia braced herself for whatever Mother had to tell her. "You're right—things shouldn't be put off. I'm not a child. You don't have to hide anything from me." It couldn't be any worse than what he'd already done. Could it?

"We had hoped you would reconcile with Troy."

Olivia looked from Mother to Gran and back. "What does Troy have to do with Father?"

"The money your father left us is gone. Mr. Ingers is demanding our rent by the end of the month."

Wait. What did money or Father have to do with Troy? She played her mother's words over in her head. Gone? Couldn't be. She knew they were low, but how could it be gone? "That can't be. We've been careful."

"Not careful enough."

"I still don't understand what that has to do with Troy."

"We had hoped you would make up with him and marry. I know it's selfish, but I didn't know what else to do." Mother was practical if nothing else.

"You want me to marry Troy to keep a roof over our heads?"

"No. I wanted you to marry the boy you've been in love with for years. Look, dear, it would be protection and support for us all."

The shame in Mother's expression twisted Olivia's heart.

"True, one benefit would be a roof. But since you are

determined to push him away, we need to consider other options." Mother believed it best to not keep secrets or a problem to herself so the whole family could work toward a resolution. "Gran and I talked about taking in wash and mending, but that still won't be enough."

"I'll help, too. We'll make it." But she saw the doubt and concern on their faces.

Chapter 5

On Friday when Troy returned from locking the safe for the weekend and releasing the teller at the end of the day, he went back to his office.

A man he'd never seen before sat in the chair opposite his desk. He wore an expensive tailored suit. Not the usual attire for a bank robber. The man stood, rising to Troy's height of six foot two, and held out his hand. "Troy Morrison?"

This could be bad. Troy was alone in the bank. If this man had nefarious plans, no one would find his body until Monday.

Mr. Jones had insisted on putting a gun in Troy's desk in the event of the unthinkable. Troy had shoved it to the far back of the drawer. Could he retrieve it without arousing suspicion in the man? He gripped the man's hand. "Yes, and you are?"

"Hewitt Raines." His suit fit too well to be concealing a gun.

A name helped Troy feel better about the situation. He rounded his desk. "What can I do for you, Mr. Raines?" He sat and glanced at the drawer that held the gun.

"Please call me Hewitt." The man chuckled. "You won't be needing that gun." He poured the bullets from his hand, dropping them onto Troy's desk one at a time. "I took them out as a precaution. I'm not here to rob the bank or cause you any trouble. But I had to wait until we could be alone."

Troy bristled at the man's brazenness. "You've done yourself no favors by rifling through my desk. I'm not inclined to be receptive to anything you have to say."

"Oh, you will."

He wouldn't. "What can I do for you?" The quicker he got this man out of the empty bank, the better.

"We have a mutual interest."

How could they? He'd never met the man before. "I doubt that."

"Violet Jones. The prettiest thing on two legs. And right pretty legs those are."

How would he know that?

"I assure you—I have no interest in Miss Jones."

"I know. I asked around town. Wasn't sure if I'd need to challenge you to a duel for the lady."

"Duel? Isn't that a bit archaic?"

"I know it's a nasty business, but Violet would enjoy men fighting over her. Honestly, I'm glad to avoid such measures."

"So how do you know Miss Jones?"

"Met her in San Francisco when she was caring for her failing grandfather this past winter. I was courting her until she caught me in a bit of a situation with another lady." He held up his hands. "A situation that wasn't my fault. You understand."

Troy actually did, but he didn't want to admit to this stranger that he had anything in common with him. And he doubted Hewitt was as innocent as he was.

"Well, Violet saw me with this other woman and has been angry with me ever since. She's just using you to make me jealous. I'm here to win her back. That's where our mutual interest lies. I want Violet, and you want a Miss Olivia Bradshaw."

How did Hewitt know about Liv? Probably when he asked around town.

"You help me get Vi back, and you are free to make up with Miss Bradshaw. She seemed distressed on Wednesday when she ran out of here."

Hewitt had seen Liv that day? "You were in the bank?"

"I was outside. So will you help me get back in Violet's good graces?"

"You're in love with Miss Jones?"

Hewitt didn't seem like the commitment type.

"I wouldn't go so far as to say *love*. But she's right pretty, and her family has a lot of money. Two things I'm looking for in a wife. If a man's going to be tied down, beauty and wealth are musts."

Troy should be upset for Violet's honor but found he couldn't. He didn't view marriage to Olivia as being "tied down." But Violet? That would be a different story. "So what is it you want me to do?"

"The party tomorrow night at the Joneses' was to be in honor of my arrival. I would propose to her, and it would turn into our engagement announcement party. Or at least I'd hoped. Then Violet's temper flared. And here I am pleading with a stranger for my future comforts."

"So you want me to let you attend the party in my stead?" He would gladly step aside. That would solve his problem and would make Liv happy.

Hewitt shook his head. "That would never do. She would be angry with both of us. Go, but be indifferent to her. Don't care one way or the other for her. Don't let on that she might have any control over you. If she gets you to be nice to her, she wins. If she gets you riled up at her, she wins."

That was a very fine line, but Troy could do it, especially if Violet shifted her focus off him. He had seen how she enjoyed holding power over others.

"I'll show up—" Hewitt thrust his arms into the air "—and declare my love for her."

Could it really be so simple? Troy grabbed on to the hope that it could and ignored the niggling doubt.

Hewitt made a fist and punched it through the air. "I could take a swing at you. Violet would like that."

Quite the conniver. "I prefer no violence."

"Are you sure? Miss Bradshaw might show you a little sympathy if you were to get hurt."

He doubted a black eye would change Liv's opinion of him. She'd just say he'd deserved it. "I'll pass."

"Suit yourself. Maybe you should take a swing at me. Then Violet could nurse me back to health." Hewitt smirked, seeming to like his idea.

Troy shook his head. "Let's do this without anyone getting hit."

"Are you sure? I don't mind having a sore jaw for a few days. Winning Violet would be well worth any amount of pain."

Sure, this plan sounded great to Hewitt. He'd have Violet's undivided attention, while Troy would likely sit in jail because Violet would insist her father press charges. And Troy would, of course, lose his job and Liv for good. "I'm not going to punch you."

Hewitt turned his hands palms up. "If you change your mind, you don't have to warn me first. I'll be ready."

Troy wouldn't change his mind. Though he did feel better about attending this supper. He would be free of Violet by the end.

He shook Hewitt's hand, locked up the bank and headed straight to Liv's to tell her the good news. He knocked on her door.

Granny Bradshaw answered with a smile. "Troy, come in."

He stepped inside. "I came to speak to Liv."

"She wasn't feeling well and went to bed early."

"She's ill? It's not anything serious, is it?"

Granny patted his arm. "Nothing that a little time won't cure. She'll come around."

"You think so?"

"Doesn't she always?"

He nodded. He would hold on to that hope. In three short days, he'd gone from the happiest man in Friday Harbor to the most miserable.

When he left and turned back toward the house, he thought he saw the curtain in Liv's window move.

Yes, hope.

The next afternoon hung heavy with unspent clouds. Olivia twirled a wild daisy as she walked beside Felicity in a meadow.

Felicity kicked at a clump of tall grass. "So you have no money? It's all gone?"

Olivia also had a hard time believing it. "We're going to take in laundry and sewing." She would likely be the one to do the washing while Mother and Gran put needle to cloth. She could already feel the painful cracks her hands would have from hours in hot water.

"Will that be enough?"

"It'll have to be. I don't know what else to do."

"You could ask Troy to—"

"No. I won't grovel to him. Not when he's having supper with another woman with no regard for my feelings." The image of Troy with Violet flashed in her mind. Deep down she knew Troy didn't care about Violet the way he did her, but there was always that small grain of doubt wearing a blister on her hope. She pushed the image aside only to have it replaced with Father's betrayal. If only Father hadn't run off, she would be able to trust Troy.

Felicity remained silent for a bit before she spoke again. "I heard the cannery is hiring."

"Really?" A job at the cannery could be the answer to Olivia's prayers. Though she loved the taste of salmon, she loathed the idea of smelling fish *all* day. "I'll go to the cannery Monday and apply."

After another bit of silence, Felicity cleared her throat. "Please don't be angry with me."

"For what?" Olivia couldn't imagine being upset at her best friend for anything.

She pointed. "Nick asked me to bring you here so he could talk to you on Troy's behalf."

Olivia looked to where Felicity indicated. A few yards in front of them, Nick stood next to a large maple tree. She stopped short. "And who is that with him?" She could see a man's trouser leg and shoe not concealed by the tree trunk.

Felicity stopped, as well.

Troy stepped out from behind the tree.

Olivia's insides flipped. She would not react to him. She would not. She had to get used to seeing him and not caring.

Planting her hands on her hips, Felicity pursed her lips. "Nicholas York, what have you done?"

He held out a hand. "Come on, Felicity. Let's leave these two to talk."

Felicity wrapped her arms around one of Olivia's. "I will not. Livia, I had no idea Troy would be here. Nick said *he* wanted to talk to you."

Olivia wanted both to run away and to hear what Troy had to say. Would it make a difference? Marrying Troy would keep a roof over her head as well as keep her out of the cannery.

Nick stepped closer and reached for Felicity. "Felicity."

Olivia gripped her friend's hands to keep her in place. She didn't trust herself to be alone with Troy and not fall into his arms for comfort as she had done many times in the months following her father's desertion.

Troy held a hand up to Nick. "That's all right. She can stay." He stepped closer.

Olivia forgot to breathe for a moment.

"Liv, you know I love you and wouldn't purposefully do anything to hurt you."

She spoke in a soft voice. "And yet you manage to time and again."

"I'm sorry for that. I suppose Felicity told you about yesterday."

Olivia glanced at her friend, whose eyes were wide, and then back to Troy.

"Apparently not. Then I will. I went to speak to Violet to talk her out of having me at the supper tonight. Felicity saw me coming out of the Joneses' home." He rushed on, "But don't blame her. It's my fault. I begged her not to tell you."

Olivia didn't care about that. All she wanted to know was if he'd succeeded at getting out of the supper.

"I asked Nick to have Felicity bring you here because I didn't know how else I could get you to see me before tonight."

Was he going to tell her or not? "I'm growing weary. What do you want to say?" She was pleased her voice didn't shake.

"Very well. A man named Hewitt Raines came to my office yesterday."

"So?"

"He wants to marry Violet."

Olivia's heart rose. Violet had another man?

"But she's angry with him. She's just using me at this party to get back at him."

Her heart and hope dipped.

"He's going to show up tonight and make his declaration to her. Then I'll be off the hook."

Olivia stared at him. He hadn't said it. "Do I understand correctly? You are still going to attend tonight?"

He held out his hands. "I have no choice. I tried everything to get out of it."

Her heart plummeted. "You are going to be there? With *her*?"

"Only until Hewitt arrives. Then I can leave."

"And what if your little plan doesn't work?"

"It will."

"What if this Hewitt Raines doesn't show up?"

"He will."

"What if Violet decides she wants to marry you instead of him?"

"She won't."

But what if she did? Olivia shook her head. "That's not good enough. I need to know that I'm more important to you than her or anything else."

"You are."

"And yet you are still attending this party."

"I'm doing this for you."

For her? "Just what every girl wants. Her beau with another woman on his arm." Her voice did shake now.

"I'm doing this to keep my job. Why can't you understand that? I love you. Why are you always so stubborn?"

"Why are you always so gullible? Do you really believe Violet is going to just turn you loose? Why should she when she can have two men under her control? She will use you over and over to make this other man jealous. I am not going to stand around waiting and watching that. Hoping that one day Violet might set you free." Tears burned her eyes.

"It's not going to be like that, Liv. I promise."

"I'm tired of promises you apparently can't keep." She pulled free of Felicity and left. She was just plain tired.

Troy watched Liv retreat with long purposeful strides.

Felicity shook her finger at Nick. "I can't believe you did this. You lied to me."

"It wasn't a lie," Nick said. "I just didn't tell you Troy would be here."

Felicity held up her hand. "I can't speak to you right now." She turned and hurried after Liv.

Troy was glad for that. He didn't want Liv to be alone. "Sorry for getting you in trouble with Felicity."

"I knew what I was doing." After a moment of silence, Nick asked, "Why?"

"Why am I going to this supper at my boss's?"

Nick shook his head. "I know why you're going, and I agree you should. You have to. Women just don't understand."

"Then what?"

"Why do you put up with Olivia? She can be difficult

at times. You could have any number of girls who would be far more compliant."

"I don't want any other girl." Liv disappeared from his sight. "The marriage vows? For better or for worse? I take those seriously."

"But you're not married yet."

"I committed my heart a long time ago to her as though I am. I promised her father I'd take care of her."

"And here I thought you were all brawn and good looks." Nick nudged him with his elbow.

"Not *all*. There's more to me."

"But not much," Nick teased.

Troy grinned and then got serious again. "I love Liv."

"I'm not sure I can see why."

Troy viewed her as his equal. She would be at his side, not trailing behind. More than a wife. A partner. She was smart, and he could discuss anything with her. "I don't know why exactly. I just do. I think I've always been in love with her. But since I was sixteen, I knew for sure." That was ten years ago. "She's spirited. Keeps me on my toes. Life is never dull with her."

"And never easy."

He'd never wanted a docile wife. He wanted Liv. "She's scared. The more she pushes me away, the more I know she needs me. I want to help and protect her."

"Scared of what?"

"Losing me. Losing her mother. Her grandmother. She hasn't always been like this. Only since her father passed away. That hit her hard. Her grandmother is old. Her mother's wheelchair bound. Her father was the robust one. The one she counted on. And he died."

"I never thought of things that way. She always seemed to be all right."

"No one saw her real hurt. No one but me. I had hoped

my steadfastness this past year would have proven to her I was going to stay by her side no matter what. I think she wants to depend on me but is afraid I'll die or something."

"I hope everything works out the way you want it to. I'm going to see if Felicity has left Olivia's."

"You really think she'll forgive you so quickly?"

Nick held out his arms as he walked backward. "I guess I'm just better at persuasion with my girl than you are with yours."

"Not likely." Troy walked with Nick. "When are you going to marry her?"

"When I get my land cleared. I'm hoping to finish up this fall. Then maybe we can marry in the spring."

"I can lend you a hand next Saturday, and maybe a few nights this week."

"I'd appreciate that."

"Tell Felicity I'm sorry. And that I coerced you." He parted ways from Nick and headed to the waterfront. Praying before going to the boardinghouse would strengthen his resolve. He'd also better pray while he dressed for the evening. An evening he hoped would be brief. Then he could stop by Liv's and tell her all was well.

Chapter 6

Olivia pushed a chunk of potato around in her stew. Had Troy eaten yet? What fancy dishes had the Joneses' cook prepared? Had Hewitt Raines already shown up and freed Troy? But if so, wouldn't he stop by her house to tell her the good news? Unless it wasn't good news. Her stomach tightened.

"Is everything all right, dear?" Mother set her spoon aside.

No, everything *wasn't* all right. Troy was with another woman. "I'm fine." She wasn't supposed to care.

"You've played more with your food than eaten it." Gran took her last bite of stew.

Olivia pushed her bowl away. "I'm not hungry."

Mother folded her hands in her lap. "Since we are all apparently done eating, we should talk."

She gave Mother her attention.

"Your grandmother went out today and found us some

work. Two private households. One needs only washing done. The other needs everything, washing, ironing, mending and sewing clothes. We had hoped to be hired by the hotel and boardinghouse, but they don't need us at the moment. If they do, they'll let us know."

"That's wonderful." Olivia twisted one hand in the other under the table. "We can ask around after church tomorrow. Maybe we can garner more work."

"That would be good. The work we've found so far won't earn us all we need and won't keep us busy for long, but it's a good start. We'll pick up the items on Monday, deliver the laundry on Wednesday and the sewing and mending on Friday." Mother seemed to have everything figured out. She glanced at Gran, who gave her a look back.

What weren't they telling her? "Is there something else?"

"The household that needs all our services..." Mother shifted her gaze away.

Olivia waited.

Mother didn't continue but looked to Gran.

"Just tell her," Gran said. "The silence isn't going to change anything."

"I'm sorry, dear."

"Sorry for what?" What had upset Mother so much?

"Jones," Gran said. "The household that need so much is the Joneses."

No, no, no. If Troy wasn't over there right now, she wouldn't mind so much working for them. This was too much to bear. Adding insult to injury.

"We don't expect you to lay a hand to any of their clothes," Mother said. "We'll have you work on other people's laundry."

Olivia stood and stacked the dishes in silence.

"Olivia?" Mother said.

"I have dishes to do." There was nothing she could say. They needed the money, so she couldn't insist that they not take the work.

She would suffer in silence. As usual.

Troy stood with his boss and four other prominent men of the Friday Harbor community. They spoke of everything from the schoolhouse and politics to the cannery and how to increase town growth. The parlor seemed less foreboding when he wasn't here alone with Violet. But he'd still rather be elsewhere.

The ladies sat across the room from the men. Violet wore a gown to match her name. She kept trying to gain his attention with a wave of her hand or a little too loudly spoken "Oh, my."

Troy purposely would not look on those occasions, but he did glance in her direction other times. Just as he was about to make eye contact with her, he would turn back to whichever man was talking and seem consumed in the conversation.

He glanced at the mantel clock. Where was Hewitt? Troy had hoped the man would show up at the start of the party so he wouldn't have to suffer through supper and the whole of the evening. He glanced at the small brass clock on the secretary desk and then the crystal tabletop one. Same time as the other clock. *Hewitt? You'd better not chicken out.* But the man *had* seemed determined.

A servant entered the parlor and announced supper.

Troy strode to the doorway, stopped, and looked back at Violet. "Are you coming?" He hoped that seemed dispassionate enough.

By the murderous expression on Violet's face, he'd succeeded. She rose and held out her hand, obviously expecting him to come to her. He simply poked out his elbow for her and waited.

As others left to enter the dining room, Violet crossed to him and squeezed his arm. "You should have come over to the settee to retrieve me."

Her grip caused only mild discomfort. Her expression? Positively entertaining. He struggled not to laugh. "Pardon my ill manners." He headed toward the dining room, propelling her to take several quick steps to keep up. He hoped this string of behaviors met with Hewitt's definition of "indifferent."

It certainly was amusing to see Violet not in control for a change.

The smell of the savory foods nauseated him. He managed to get the first two courses down, but by the third one, he doubted Hewitt would appear at all.

Beside him, Violet pivoted to face him and smiled sweetly. "You're not eating your shoulder of lamb."

"My appetite seems to have waned." He took a sip of water from his crystal goblet.

Her fork clinked against her plate, and she spoke in a hushed tone. "Don't think I'll put up with you claiming some sort of ailment to be excused from this evening."

He let his mouth curl up on the corners. "I wouldn't dream of excusing myself." He would wait to be asked to leave after Hewitt arrived. He hoped that would be soon.

He'd eaten most of his lamb by the time that course was removed. As the next course was being served, a commotion erupted at the front entry.

"Violet!" a mournful voice called.

Violet's eyes widened as recognition registered in her expression.

About time.

She jumped to her feet, as did all the men around the table, including Troy.

He, for one, was glad to get this little drama over with.

Violet clutched his arm. "Come."

He let her pull him along.

Dripping wet, Hewitt stood near the front door.

Violet tightened her hold on Troy's arm. "Mr. Raines, whatever are you doing here?"

Hewitt had been right. This was exactly what Violet wanted. To be on the arm of another man for Hewitt to see. She was a master manipulator. Something Liv was not. But Violet was too young and naive to realize Hewitt was far more seasoned in the art.

The man fell to his knees in front of her. "Violet, my love. I've come to beg you to take me back."

She turned her face away from him and raised her chin. "As you can see, you are as easily replaced as a pair of shoes."

Hewitt took her free hand in both of his. "Forgive me. Take me back. I can't live another day without you."

The man might be overdoing it.

Violet loosened her hold on Troy's arm.

Evidently, Hewitt knew Violet well.

Troy wasn't sure if he should say anything. Should he argue or tell Hewitt to leave?

Disinterest.

Saying nothing would show that best.

She waved a delicate hand in Hewitt's general direction as though he were nothing more than refuse. "Troy, tell this man to leave."

That was the last thing he wanted to do. "The poor sap is drenched."

With a huffed breath, Violet pulled her hands free of both men and folded her arms. "I wish for you to leave."

Evidently she needed more pleading.

"I'll prove my devotion to you." Hewitt stood and raised his fists toward Troy. "I'll fight for you."

Troy took a step back. Certainly they didn't need to resort to a physical fight.

To her credit, Violet moved in front of Troy and spoke to Hewitt. "I will not tolerate violence."

"As you wish." Hewitt glanced at Troy to do something as he let his hands fall to his sides.

But what should he do?

"Leave." Violet pointed.

Lowering his head, Hewitt backed toward the door. "This wound will never heal, even if I live to be a hundred."

No.

Hewitt had to stay. Troy was the one who needed to leave.

The man sidestepped off the area carpet and onto the wet marble floor. His arms windmilled as his feet lost their grip.

But Troy could tell that the man had himself under control as he landed and let himself fall back so his head hit the floor. But not too hard. His eyes closed.

Troy could see the playacting for what it was only because he knew to look for it. Everyone else seemed fooled.

In a swish of fabric, Violet rushed over and knelt. "Hewitt, are you all right? Speak to me." She cradled his head on her lap. His wet hair made dark patches on her dress.

Hewitt's eyes fluttered open, and his lips moved as though he wanted to speak but didn't. His eyelids closed.

"Hewitt, darling. Can you hear me?"

He opened his eyes again and touched her cheek with a finger. "Violet? Is that you?"

"Yes, darling." Violet smiled and then raised her gaze. "Father, we need to get him into bed and call for the doctor."

The butler and Mr. Jones helped Hewitt to his feet and assisted him up the stairs. Violet followed.

That had been brilliant. Troy was tempted to applaud the performance but refrained lest he give the man away.

"Violet?" Troy asked. "Shall I take my leave?"

"I think that's best."

Troy stepped outside onto the covered porch and let the cool rain-drenched air refresh him. Freedom.

He walked through the drizzle to Liv's. It was late. The lights were all extinguished. He would see her tomorrow.

He wished she hadn't gone to sleep not knowing the outcome of the evening.

Olivia wearily opened the front door Sunday morning and stopped short. What was *he* doing here? Although she already knew.

Troy pushed away from the porch's support post, doffed his cap and bowed. "Good morning, ladies. Your coach awaits." He swept his arm backward toward the waiting buggy. Every Sunday he rented that buggy and escorted them to church.

She hadn't been sure if she would be able to manage getting Mother to church without him. "I wasn't expecting you this morning."

"Liv, you know me better than that."

That she did. She had hoped and prayed he wouldn't show up. Was there nothing she could say to deter him? Seeing him made getting over him that much harder. But she would have been disappointed if he hadn't come. Had his plan worked last night?

He dodged around her and wheeled her mother out and down the ramp at the side of the porch he and Father had built after Mother's accident. He lifted Mother easily into the backseat and went around to help Gran in beside her.

Oh, no. That left Olivia up front with him. "Gran, you ride in the front. I'll sit back here with Mother."

Gran waved her hand in the air. "Nonsense. I prefer the back."

"You can see better up front."

Gran gave Olivia a pointed look. "Don't argue with me, young lady."

Olivia caught Troy's triumphant smile as he helped Gran into the back. Like Troy, Gran was not easily deterred.

"You are such a nice boy," Gran said. "Don't you think so, Olivia?" Gran was plotting against her. She did have a sweet spot for Troy.

Troy could be quite charming when he wanted to be. The problem was he wanted to be with every woman over the age of consent. He had a way of making any woman feel special.

He held his hand out to her.

She stared, contemplating declining his offer. It would serve no purpose to refuse and risk falling in the muddy street. Not that a little dirt would harm her gray calico dress that matched the sky and her mood.

She placed her hand in his no longer than absolutely necessary. "Thank you."

He put Mother's wheelchair on the back of the buggy and climbed up front beside her. "I know why you wore that dress."

He couldn't possibly.

"You think it makes you unattractive. But you are beautiful no matter what you wear."

Her mouth turned up in response to his compliment. But she quickly tamed it. He had been wrong about her reason. None of her other dresses with color in them appealed to her anymore. The drab dress mirrored her bruised emotions. "Mr. Morrison, you may save your breath. Your flattery no longer holds sway over me."

"Oh, but I think it does. How else will you know I'm sweet on you?"

Unbelievable. "Oh, I don't know. Maybe by staying out of other ladies' arms."

"I told you that wasn't my fault. You sure know how to throw a bucket of cold water on a moment." He snapped the reins.

Unfortunately, Troy had given her too many opportunities. She wished he hadn't.

Anyway, she was done with dithering. She had made up her mind to work at the cannery. So the matter of her heart was settled.

After the service, in the churchyard, Troy left Mrs. Bradshaw and Granny Bradshaw with a gaggle of ladies. He took Liv's arm and led her away from the others, not letting her mild protest stop him. He pointed at Hewitt with Violet securely attached to his arm. "See there. That's Violet's fiancé."

"Him?"

"Do you know Mr. Raines?"

"No. Of course not. I've seen him around town."

As long as Hewitt didn't start flirting with Liv. "See how happy Violet is with him?"

"I'm delighted for her." Her tone ran counter to her statement.

"This nonsense with Violet is over." Couldn't she see there was nothing to be jealous of?

She pulled free and faced him. "You still don't get it. It's not Violet. It's not even the dozen other women who flirt with you."

It sure seemed that way to him.

"It's you."

"Me? I can't control what they do."

"But you can control what you do." Her voice held no emotion. "You don't try, even a little bit, to discourage any of them. That's why Violet was able to use you. You don't learn."

He'd learned. Violet would never get the better of him again.

"You don't care that it hurts me when women flirt with you, and you do nothing about it." Her arms hung limply at her sides.

"I care."

"Well, I don't. You do whatever you like. With whomever you like." She walked away.

Gooseflesh prickled his skin. Liv was different this time. Dispassionate. Her voice had been flat as though she really didn't care. Had he truly lost her this time? He hurried to catch up. "Liv, please. I promise to rebuff any woman who comes near me."

"I have more important concerns than to fret over what you are up to."

"Please don't give up on me."

"Not you. Us. I have put my hopes in us for far too long. It's not going to work. I can't continue this way."

"I can change." The look in her eyes told him he didn't believe him.

"Can you see to it that Mother and Gran make it home?"

"Of course. You know I will."

"Thank you. I wish you all the best." She walked away.

He watched her retreat. Hopefully not forever. Suffering her wrath was far easier to take than this detached version of Liv. Her anger had let him know she still cared. Deeply.

He would just need to find a way to get her riled up at him. Then he would know. Then he could go on.

Olivia hurried away from Troy. It had been all she could manage to not break down, cry, and let him comfort her as he'd done numerous times after Father left.

The tears welled now and spilled onto her cheeks.

She loved Troy but didn't really trust him. Without threat of her anger, would something less innocent happen between him and another woman?

He wanted to marry her and take care of her. He knew that meant taking on the responsibility of Mother and Gran, as well. And yet he was willing.

Should she let him? Just to ensure a roof over her head? While her heart broke daily? Once he had her as his wife, he would have no need for discretion. Could she live that way?

As she hurried home, she prayed for guidance. The only thought that followed was *Troy loves you*. She was sure of his love, but could she be sure of his fidelity?

At home, she opened windows and the back door to let the breeze cool the house. Then she picked peas and scallions to have with dinner. She had the meal started when she heard hoofbeats stop out front. Mother and Gran were home.

And with them…Troy.

He always stayed for Sunday dinner. A way of thanking him for taking them to church.

She corralled her emotions and met the trio at the door.

Troy's face showed surprise at her presence. He stared, evidently not knowing what to say.

"Olivia, here you are," Mother said. "You just up and disappeared."

Olivia forced a smile. "I wanted to get dinner started. It will be ready shortly."

Mother reached back and patted Troy's hand on the back of her wheelchair. "You're staying for dinner."

"I..."

Olivia kept her gaze on Mother lest her well-confined emotions break free. "Of course he is. Go on into the parlor, and I'll finish up." She strode back into the kitchen. She would show Troy—as well as Mother and Gran—that she and Troy were no more. She could be civil.

The strain around the table tainted the food.

After the meal, Troy said, "I should be going."

Gran spoke up. "You don't have to leave yet."

Troy looked pointedly at Olivia. "I don't want to overstay my welcome."

"You are always welcome here," Mother said.

"Just the same, I should go."

Gran waved a hand at Olivia. "See him to the door."

She didn't want to but rose anyway and escorted him to the door. "Thank you for delivering us to church and bringing Mother and Gran home."

He scooped up her hand.

The heat of his touch nearly undid her, but she didn't pull her hand away. Though she longed for this small intimacy, she couldn't let him know.

He caressed the back of her hand with his thumb. "I have not given up on us. I have enough faith for both of us. I have prayed every day for the past year that everything would be right between us. We will be together. I will wait however long it takes."

Oh. That was so sweet. She wanted to believe every word, but then the image of him with Violet spoiled it.

With a deep bow, he kissed her hand.

Her knees went weak. "I want to trust you."

He looked up with his dimpled smile.

And she saw all the women he'd ever smiled at. She chided herself for being so easily drawn into his charm. She pulled her hand free. "But I can't."

"That you want to is enough for now." He walked away.

She was a silly ninny. She shouldn't have said that. She had unwittingly given him hope. Now he would try harder to win her affections. Or at least get her to confess her affections.

He would see soon enough that she would stand her ground.

Chapter 7

The next day, Troy sat across his desk from Widow Cornwall. This had been a profitable meeting. She was still young, beautiful and wealthy. She would attract another husband in no time. Until then, she needed someone trustworthy to handle her money.

Mr. Jones had taken to having Troy assist all the ladies, young, old, single, or married, unless they had a jealous husband. He said that Troy could charm a skunk out of its bad odor and a mule out of its stubbornness. Providing it was a female skunk or mule.

Troy came around his desk and proffered his hand to Mrs. Cornwall.

She took his offered assistance and rose. "I always feel safe in your hands and my money in your care."

"I'm honored."

"If your heart wasn't already taken, I'd cast my net for you."

Troy smiled. "I'm flattered. If my heart wasn't already securely in another's hands, I just might let myself get caught in your net." But he never would.

Though the widow was his age, she didn't appeal to him. It was good business to allow her, and other ladies like her, to believe there could be a spark of hope even when there was none. He opened the door for her.

She leaned forward and gave him a peck on the cheek. "That girl of yours is a fortunate lady."

He wished Liv thought so. He stepped out of his office with Mrs. Cornwall.

Liv stared directly at him. She had seen.

As he passed Liv on his way escorting Mrs. Cornwall to the exit door, he said, "I can explain." He knew he could get her to understand. She was smart. She understood business dealings. "Please wait right there."

"You are just like my father," Olivia said in a low voice.

Normally, he would take her statement as a compliment. But the way she said it made it sound like something bad. Wasn't being like her father a good thing? And what did her father have to do with this situation?

He continued to the door, opened it, and motioned to Mrs. Cornwall's driver.

She stopped before getting into her carriage. "Miss Bradshaw is pretty. I hope she knows how fortunate she is to hold your heart."

Tears burned Olivia's eyes. She blinked several times to stave them off. To think she'd come to make amends with Troy. She'd decided not to punish him for Violet's improprieties. But maybe Saturday's supper party wasn't fully Violet's fault.

Troy cupped her elbow. "Let's go into my office."

She went with him. "You just can't help yourself, can you?"

"Liv, that wasn't what it looked like." He closed the door. "It didn't mean anything. I promise."

"That's where you're wrong. It did mean something. It meant something to her." She pointed toward the door. "Because you don't discourage them, they all think they might have a chance with you."

"Well, every one of them is wrong. I'm all yours."

"But they don't know that. You have given them hope. And that is what hurts. Your ego is more important than me."

"I thought the more other women wanted me, the more appealing I'd be to you."

How ridiculous! "No. A woman wants to know her man is all hers. That she is enough for him. But I guess I'm not." She turned to leave.

He gripped her hand. "You *are* enough for me. I didn't know. Give me another chance."

"I don't know if I can." Her heart couldn't take any more. "You used up all your chances."

"Please don't say that."

She pulled her hand free. "I can't do this anymore with you, Troy. I just can't." She turned to the door and opened it.

"I haven't given up. I will win you back."

She wasn't sure if she even wanted him to try. She slipped out the door and hurried out of the bank. How could her life have turned on its head in the span of a week? From reconciliation with Troy to hopeless and destitute.

Her mission had been twofold. If the first part went well, she wouldn't need to pursue the second part. But now off she went to the second part.

By the time she reached the cannery, her queasy stomach had done battle with her scant breakfast. When she entered the building, the odor of fish accosted her. She regretted eating.

A boy of twelve escorted her to an office.

William Ecker, assistant to the manager of the cannery, sat behind a desk. When he looked up and saw her, he rose from his chair. He stood nearly as tall as Troy, though he was not as fit. He was handsome with a gentle smile. His hair was combed so neatly not a hair dare be out of place. "What have I done to be honored with a visit?"

Relief at having him there settled her stomach a bit. She saw him at church each Sunday. He had always been kind. "I hear the cannery is hiring."

"Have a seat." He pointed. "Please don't tell me you've come to work."

She sat with her back straight. "I have."

He smiled and stepped from behind his desk. "Shouldn't you be married and halfway to having your second or third child by now?"

Her face warmed at the implication and the poke at her age. "I am in need of employment."

"What does Troy have to say about this?"

Her breath caught at the mention of his name. "He has no say in matters that concern me." But he would have plenty to say if he knew.

"I see." Mr. Ecker sat on the corner of his desk, facing her. "I thought there was a chill between the two of you yesterday at church. Are you done with him?"

Her heart said no. "I don't see how that is relevant to my purpose for being here."

"It's a simple enough question." He studied her.

She shifted under his scrutiny. "Yes, we're through."

Like the sun is through rising and setting. At least be honest with yourself.

She pushed the stray thoughts down with others like them to where they couldn't nag her.

He spread his arms. "Why do you want to work here?"

Desperation. She needed time to sort through her feelings for Troy. A month or two of rent would afford her that time. Wouldn't it? "Are you hiring or not?"

He chuckled. "We are." He hesitated.

She heard a "but" coming.

"But I will make you a better offer." His features softened. "If you are truly done with Troy Morrison, I offer you my hand in marriage." He held out his hand, palm up to her.

She jerked to her feet, causing the chair to scrape the floor. "What?"

"You shouldn't be working. You are a lady who should be taken care of. If Troy won't marry you, I will. I assure you my offer is genuine."

She couldn't believe he just proposed. Just like that. No pomp. No tradition. No romance at all. Practical. Mother would like that.

He thrust his arms out from his sides. "Come now, Olivia. You can't be that shocked."

But she *was* shocked.

"You're unmarried, good-natured, and beautiful, and I'm a bachelor who has the means to take care of you. The men still outnumber the women this far west. How you have remained unwed is astonishing. I will be moving up to the position of manager in a year or two. We would be all set. You would want for nothing."

We? She had never entertained the idea of marrying anyone but Troy. When Troy spoke of marriage or their future, it set her heart dancing. But Mr. Ecker's proposal caused a ripple of trepidation through her. Not that he wasn't a nice man. Marriage to anyone other than Troy held no appeal. And since she wasn't going to marry him…"I'm flattered, but I'm not interested in marriage. If there are no positions, I'll be on my way." She scooted toward the door.

"Don't run off. I'll hire you. We always need girls on the floor." He remained seated on the corner of the desk.

She stopped and stared at him.

He moved back around his desk and indicated the chair she had vacated. "Please sit."

When she did, he sat, as well.

"Right now I only have packing positions available. In a week or two, I can probably move you to labeling. You'll like that much better."

He was promising her favors after she had declined his proposal?

He opened a ledger and spoke as he wrote. "O…liv…ia Brad…shaw. Address?" He glanced up. "I need it for our records. If I wanted to make a social call, I know how to get to your house. This town isn't that big."

He wasn't thinking of doing *that*, was he?

She told him her address as well as the additional information he requested.

"When would you like to start?"

"As soon as possible."

"Today?"

"Yes." She hadn't imagined things would work out quite this well or so quickly.

He made a notation, closed the ledger, and stood. "Then come with me."

She followed him out.

The canning room bustled with shifting and rolling

cans, clattering machinery and people. The smell of fish was far more pungent. She resisted the urge to plug her nose. She would have to get used to it. Breathing through her mouth, she followed him in.

Mr. Ecker waved a girl over. "Sally, this is Olivia. She is starting today. Show her how to pack the cans."

"Yes, sir." Sally couldn't be more than seventeen. "Come with me." She handed Olivia an apron and a pair of sleeve guards.

Olivia followed and was soon stuffing cooked salmon into one tin can after another. After a couple of hours, the lunch whistle blew. She hadn't been prepared to stay when she came this morning. She was tired and hungry. And she hadn't even worked a full day.

The girls removed their soiled aprons and sleeve guards and shuffled toward the door. Sally turned to Olivia. "Are you coming? We eat outside when it's not raining."

She couldn't sit with them, having nothing to eat. "I need to use the privy."

"All right."

Olivia watched the girl disappear with the others.

"How did it go?"

She gasped and spun around to face Mr. Ecker. "Fine."

"Come with me."

"Where?"

"To eat."

"The others went outside."

"But you are not. You brought no food with you this morning."

"I'm fine." Her stomach growled.

He grinned. "I hear otherwise. You weren't expecting to stay all day. I can't have you fainting in the middle of the afternoon." He took two paces.

She didn't follow.

He stopped. "You are a stubborn one. Either follow me or go home and don't come back."

She couldn't do that, so she followed.

On his desk sat two covered plates.

"I order in from the hotel dining room. I took the liberty of having a plate sent over for you."

"I can't accept this."

"I'm only trying to be considerate, Olivia."

She stared at the covered dish, wondering what was under it while her mouth watered.

He guided her to the chair and removed the lid. Roast beef, mashed potatoes with gravy, a roll, and green beans. "It's already paid for, so don't let it go to waste."

She sat. "Thank you." She offered up a quick silent blessing for the food and picked up the fork.

After she had eaten half her meal, she glanced up.

Mr. Ecker wasn't eating. He was staring. At her.

"What?"

"Are you ready to quit and accept my proposal?"

She squared her shoulders. "No, I'm not." She might not be used to this kind of labor, but she wasn't some debutante who'd never done any work. The money would go a long way toward paying rent.

"Shall I send a message to your mother, letting her know where you are and not to expect you until supper? So she won't worry."

Something else she'd forgotten to do. "That would be kind of you."

He wrote on a fresh sheet of paper and folded it. "Christopher?"

The boy who had escorted her in this morning appeared at the doorway.

Mr. Ecker held out the paper. "Take this to Miss Bradshaw's residence." He gave the boy directions. "Wait for any reply they might have and report to me at once."

"Yes, sir." The boy snatched the paper and ran off.

"I'll let you know if they send any word back."

"Thank you. I should return to work." She pushed up from the chair.

He stood, as well. "It's not quite time. You haven't finished your meal."

"I'm sorry for being wasteful, but I'm quite satisfied. Thank you."

"Shall I walk you down?"

"I can find my way." It would do her no good for the other workers to think she was getting special favors. Even though she was.

Olivia arrived back in the packing room as the others entered from an exterior door.

Sally tied on her apron. "Where did you go?"

"Mr. Ecker needed to speak to me."

"Mercy. Doesn't the man know you needed to eat?"

"No worry. I ate."

At the end of the day, Olivia's feet and legs had nearly gone numb from standing. Her arms, shoulders and back ached. Places she didn't know could hurt, hurt. Was there any part of her not in pain?

She would get used to it. She had to.

Mr. Ecker met her as she was leaving the packing room. "I'll walk you out."

Sally gave her a sideways look and scuttled away.

Olivia wished he wouldn't show her any undue attention. "You don't have to do that."

"I want to. Come along now."

Outside, she stopped short. A buggy waited. Presumably his.

He faced her. "Do you know what I like most about your working here?"

She couldn't imagine. "I'm tired. I just want to get home so I can make supper."

He laid an open hand on his chest. "I offer you my service as driver. Let me give you a ride. I have my buggy right here." He motioned behind him.

The ride might give him the wrong impression. "That's very generous, but I think it's best if I walk."

But before she could take a step, he continued. "What I like about your working here is that it gives me a chance to ingratiate myself to you."

Ingratiate himself? She never would have imagined William Ecker was interested in her. She'd only ever had eyes for Troy. But William was a lot like Troy. Tall, handsome, charming, and not easily deterred. But a lot less insistent than Troy. He would be far easier to put off, not having the same history of expectations with her that Troy did.

"I'm flattered, but let me save you some trouble. I came only to work, *not* to find a husband. I don't want to give you the wrong impression."

He dipped his head. "Perhaps for now."

She caught a glint in his eye. Maybe he would be as insistent as Troy, after all.

Troy fisted his hands at the sight of Liv talking to William Ecker outside the cannery. Though he stood across the street some distance away, there was no mistaking what he saw. What were those two doing together? William seemed to be offering Liv a ride in his buggy.

Don't accept, Liv. Don't. The thought of her in the company of another man tore at his insides. Was this how

Liv felt when she saw him interacting with other ladies? This twisting inside? A gnawing sensation?

Liv walked away.

Finally.

But William did not. He stood, watching Liv.

Stop it.

Troy strode up the street and cut across on another road. His step faltered at the sight of Liv's hunched shoulders and her limp arms hanging at her sides. He hurried up to her. "Hello, Liv."

She sucked in a startled breath. "Troy." She straightened her entire frame and pushed her mouth into a slight smile. "Fancy seeing you about in this part of town."

"I work not so far from here. Is everything all right?"

"Of course. I'm fine, just fine." She pulled at her sleeves.

Now he knew something was wrong. "Your mother and grandmother are well?"

"Yes. Why do you ask?"

"You aren't normally out this time of day."

She waved her hand. "We are all just fine. Nothing to worry about."

There *was* something to worry about. Though he didn't know what. "Are you headed home?"

"Yes."

"I'll walk you then."

She spoke too brightly. "I wouldn't want to trouble you."

"No trouble."

"Honestly, you don't have to."

What was she hiding? "Why not?"

She hesitated, obviously trying to come up with a feasible excuse. "Because."

Because was what one said when one didn't have a

real answer. Or didn't want to give a sincere response. "Because of William Ecker?"

She stopped and stared at the ground. "What?"

He knew she'd heard him. "I saw the two of you. Why were you meeting with William?"

She gave a schoolgirl giggle and pulled at the cuff of her blouse. "Nonsense. I wasn't meeting with him. I merely ran into him and said hello." She continued walking.

He matched her pace and tucked her hand into the crook of his elbow. "Then you won't mind my walking you home."

A moment passed before she answered. "Of course not."

No rebuff? No attempt to pull her hand free? And why did she smell so strongly of fish? He suspected that if he asked, he would get another noncommittal answer.

She chattered almost nervously the whole way to her house.

What was wrong? She wasn't herself. What had happened to her fire? Her witty remarks? She was cordial and polite, reminiscent of the Liv from two years ago, but without the spark of life she used to have.

He wouldn't press the matter now. He stopped at the street end of her walkway.

She slipped her hand from his arm. "Will you be staying for supper? I'm afraid it will be a bit. I lost track of the time and haven't started cooking yet."

"I can't. I promised Nick I'd go over to his place and help him out."

"Oh." She almost sounded disappointed.

"Nick's hoping to get his land cleared this fall so after he plants in the spring, he can marry Felicity."

"She will be so happy about that."

He took her hand and kissed it. "Maybe another time for supper?"

"Certainly." She headed up her walk.

Again no rebuff.

Regardless of her grit, she was obviously tired. He stared after her. He would figure out why.

On her porch, Olivia turned to see Troy still standing at the end of the walk. She'd appreciated having his arm for support. She'd only slept in fits last night in anticipation of going to the cannery today.

She wanted to run back to him and insist he stay for supper. Did she want Troy or not? Did she trust him or not? Yes, no. No, yes. A jumble of confusion bounced around inside her.

Troy doffed his cap and gave a sweeping bow with it.

She waved back. She wanted to let him take care of her, but for all the wrong reasons. Fear of losing him? A roof? Not having to work at the cannery?

He strolled off down the street.

Come back, her heart whispered.

She opened her front door to the smell of supper cooking. Bless Gran's and Mother's hearts. She hadn't expected the two of them to cook, but she was grateful they had.

Her arms were heavy with fatigue as she raised them to remove her hat. It had taken all the energy she had left not to faint into Troy's arms. To let him comfort and soothe her.

Mother wheeled up to where Olivia still stood by the door. "The cannery?"

Olivia didn't need a lecture right now. "We need the money. With the sewing, laundry and cannery money, we might have enough for rent." She gripped the handle on Mother's chair and pushed. "Supper smells good."

"We thought it was the least we could do with you working all day. How did it go?"

"Fine." She didn't elaborate on how tired she was or how her whole body hurt. Or the odor of fish she'd never be able to scrub off. She couldn't actually smell the fish any longer. Her nose had probably been permanently damaged so she would never smell things right again.

She'd pretended she didn't reek of fish while Troy walked with her. She hoped he hadn't noticed. But how could he not?

Sitting at the table, she nearly nodded off while Mother said grace. She would get used to this work. She would.

When she'd finished eating, she cleared away the dirty dishes. In the corner of the kitchen, a mound of laundry awaited her.

Mother hurried in. "We couldn't get the clothesline strung up in here. If you can do that, Gran and I will wash the clothes." Father had attached a series of hooks high on the kitchen walls for rainy days.

"Mother, you've tried to do wash before." Olivia rolled up one sleeve and then the other. "It doesn't work well from your chair. You end up as wet as the laundry. Your talents are best used with a needle and thread." Mother could make the smallest stitches and mend a tear so that it was almost invisible. "And the last time Gran hunched over the washtub, she was laid up in bed for a week because of her back. I'll do the wash."

Mother stretched out her arm. "Olivia, wait." She glanced at the pile of laundry.

Olivia held up a hand. "It's best if I don't know." If she

could pretend none of these clothes belonged to Violet, the chore would be much more bearable.

"The water's hot on the stove." Gran gave her a look of sympathy.

"I appreciate that." As Olivia hauled the washtub across the floor, her sore muscles protested. She shaved off pieces of lye soap from the bar into the tub, dumped in the hot water, and added several items of clothing. She opened the cupboard where they kept the indoor clothesline and set the cording on the counter. Then she started with the supper dishes.

As she washed dishes and clothes and strung the line, her mind wandered back to Troy time and again. No matter how much she told herself not to, he was always in her next thought.

She didn't know where her second wind had come from, but she was only halfway through the pile when she ran out of clothesline. All the washing was a nice change from her day's work at the cannery and had seemed to remove the salmon smell from her hands and arms. She dried her hands and went into the parlor, where Mother and Gran busily sewed.

Mother looked up. "Are you through, dear?"

Olivia shook her head. "The line is full. I'll take them down in the morning and wash a few more things before I head off to the cannery. I'll wash the rest tomorrow night. What can I help with?"

"You've done enough for one day. Off to bed." Mother waved her away.

She appreciated that. "Good night." Now that she had nothing to do, her second wind rushed out of her. With great effort, she lifted one foot and then the other to keep her feet from scuffing the floor and giving away her exhaustion.

Once in her room, pulling off her clothes took the last of her energy. She fell into bed. Visions of Troy with Violet danced through her thoughts. She wasn't sure if she cared anymore.

Maybe that was best.

Chapter 8

On Wednesday, Troy waited and watched from a distance. For the third day in a row, Liv and William spoke at the end of the workday. Was she meeting him? On purpose?

Had she truly thrown Troy over for another man? Had she indeed had enough of him?

Nothing had happened between her and William as far as Troy could tell. He never took her hand. She never rode in his buggy. But something was going on between them.

He remembered this same possessive, jealous feeling from eight years ago when several boys started paying Liv more attention. Though at that point, he'd known for two years that he wanted to marry her, she'd been too young to be courted. So he'd waited, until others took an interest in her. Now he had that same sickening gut reaction that he might lose Liv to another man. She'd always come back to him. Had this time been one time too many for her?

No.

He would win her back. He had to.

Liv walked away, and William watched her. He needed to stop doing that.

Right now.

Once Liv was far enough up the street, Troy crossed to William, who *still* stared after her.

"What is your interest in Miss Bradshaw?" He didn't care that his voice had a harsh tone to it.

"Hello, Troy." William gave him a pleasant smile. "I take an interest in all my employees."

"Employee?"

"Olivia started at the cannery on Monday. She didn't tell you?"

She hadn't. "And your interest in her? It's more than just as her employer."

William eyed him a moment. "You sound like a jealous man."

That's because he was. "Wouldn't you be if another man was showing your girl attention?"

"She said the two of you had parted ways."

She'd said that? She must be angrier than he realized.

"Well, we haven't."

William glanced up the street in the direction Liv had gone. "Does she know that?"

Evidently not. "She just needs a little time." Time he'd always been willing to give her. Until now.

William studied him a moment. "Very well. But I won't wait long."

Troy appreciated that. He'd hoped she would have come around once the dinner party was over but apparently not.

Why was she working anyway?

He would have to figure a way to talk her out of this job.

And to get back into her good graces.

On Friday afternoon, Troy recorded deposit amounts from the teller's slips into the ledger. He had watched Liv grow more and more tired as the week wore on. He suspected she took the position at the cannery to show him she could build a life of her own without him. There was nothing wrong with her doing so, but he wanted them to build a life together.

Jack poked his head in. "Customer to see you, sir."

Troy closed the slips inside the ledger and rose. "Send him in."

The office boy disappeared, and Nick appeared in the doorway.

Troy stepped out from behind his desk and shook Nick's hand. "I wasn't expecting you."

Nick smiled but said nothing and closed the door. When he turned back, his casual demeanor had been replaced with a serious expression.

Troy hoped nothing was terribly wrong. "Have a seat." He motioned as he sat.

Nick pulled up the chair and leaned forward. "Felicity is concerned for Olivia."

"I am, too. She's exhausting herself with this foolish job she's taken to prove something to me. I'm just not sure what."

"It's not about you this time."

Troy doubted that. Liv's actions had been spurred by something he'd said or done for as long as he could remember. She wanted a reaction from him. Sometimes he obliged, and sometimes he did not. He didn't want her to think she had total sway over him.

But this time seemed different. This time she was more resolute. This time could split them, especially if William got in the way. She had a burr under her saddle that went beyond Violet. Once he figured out what it was, he could remove it, and all would be well again.

Nick continued. "Their landlord is demanding their rent by the end of the month or else they have to leave."

He hadn't known they were having financial difficulties. "Leave? Where would they go?"

Nick shook his head. "Even with Olivia working, they won't likely have the money."

"How do you know this?"

"Olivia told Felicity, who told me. I came right over."

"So that's why she's working. Why didn't she come to me?"

Nick raised an eyebrow.

"Right. She's angry with me again." Or so she would like everyone to believe.

"Don't tell her I told you."

"Because Felicity wasn't supposed to tell you, and you weren't supposed to tell me."

Nick nodded. "Regardless of what the ladies think, I knew you should be told."

"I appreciate that. I'll talk to her on Sunday." If he made a special visit, she might realize how he gained this information. He didn't want Nick or Felicity to receive a scolding.

After Nick left, Troy opened the cover of the accounts ledger, contemplating doing something he never did. Snooping into a customer's account for personal reasons. He'd purposely stayed away from the Bradshaws' account. It hadn't seemed right to be privy to their exact balance.

But because Liv was putting herself at risk, he needed to know how bad it really was. Maybe they had money in their account and weren't aware of it. It had been months since Liv came into the bank for business.

He took a deep breath and turned the page. He stared in disbelief.

Zero? How could they not have any money whatsoever?

On Saturday, Olivia stood over the washtub, scrubbing their own laundry. It had been a long tiring week. Monday evening had brought rain that lasted through Tuesday evening. So when she'd washed the laundry they'd been hired to do, she had to hang it across the kitchen to dry overnight. Not ideal, but it worked. Then Mother and Gran ironed it and worked on mending while she was at the cannery. She hated that Mother and Gran had to toil so hard in their conditions.

Wednesday, after a full day at the cannery, she'd delivered the laundry and the completed mending. Thursday evening, she helped with the mending and sewing. Friday evening, she delivered the remainder of the mending and sewing while collecting next week's work.

And by Thursday, Mr. Ecker must have realized her fortitude and that she wasn't interested in him. He had stopped escorting her out of the cannery and offering her a ride. So tired by Friday, she wished he hadn't. She would have liked a ride to rest her tired feet and body.

She scrubbed and scrubbed the clothes she'd worn to the cannery all week, but they still smelled of fish. Maybe the sun beating down on them would cast out the odor, but mist hung in the air like a curtain. So she draped the skirt and blouse over the line stretched across the kitchen.

Gran spoke in a sugary tone. "You have a visitor."

That could only mean one person.

Could she will him away? She was too tired to resist his charm. Taking a deep breath, she swiveled around.

Troy stood in the doorway next to Gran. "I've come to take you for a carriage ride."

"That's very kind, but I have work to complete." She was pleased she hadn't snapped and had actually sounded pleasant.

"Come now." Gran motioned her forward. "You've done plenty of work. Go enjoy yourself."

Enjoy? Was that even possible anymore? "It's raining."

"Just a light drizzle." Troy flashed his dimpled smile. "I've borrowed Nick's trap."

Gran took Olivia's hand and placed it on Troy's arm. "I won't let you do any more work until you have rested a bit. Now go."

"Well, if it's rest I need, then I should lie down."

Troy covered her hand. "You can rest while you're sitting in the buggy." He pulled her along.

Gran draped a shawl around Olivia's shoulders, and Troy took her blue and white-lace umbrella from the stand.

She hadn't the strength or energy to resist either of them. A respite would be welcome.

Outside, Troy opened the umbrella and held it over them.

She stopped midway down the brick path and faced him. "Only a few minutes. I have work to do." She didn't relish all that needed to be done and wished she could put it off. But tomorrow was the day of rest. And rest she would with a nice nap in the afternoon.

He nodded his assent, guided her to the two-wheeled carriage and helped her in. He turned the rig around on the street and headed down into town.

The rhythmic clomping of the horse's hooves and the swaying of the buggy pulled at her eyelids.

Troy reined in the horse down by the waterfront and set the brake. He and Liv had sat in a rig similar to this many times. Sometimes to view the sunset, sometimes to watch raindrops make tiny rings in the harbor.

Today, they would do neither. Liv's head had lolled to the side and rested on his shoulder.

He shifted her enough to put his arm around her shoulders to both keep her warm and to support her better while she slept. She was wearing herself out. But at least now he knew why.

Unable to wait until Sunday to talk to her, he'd figured a buggy ride was the perfect ruse. He hadn't anticipated she'd be so worn-out from the week that she wouldn't be able to stay awake. She obviously needed the rest, and he wouldn't disturb her.

He settled back in the seat and listened to her even breathing. He would enjoy this time of peace with her. For when she woke, she likely wouldn't be too happy with him. So he would pretend all was well between them for now.

In time, she would forget about the supper with Violet and forgive him. But he sensed that her resistance to him was something more. He would figure out what and fix that, as well.

After half an hour, Troy knew it wouldn't be proper to stay any longer. With his free hand, he managed to grip the reins, release the brake, and turn the horse back up the road. When he reined in at Liv's house, she still hadn't woken. He put it off a few minutes longer, enjoying the serenity.

The time had come to bear the consequences of letting her sleep. He kissed the top of her head. "Liv?"

Though her breathing changed, she didn't stir.

He jostled her. "Liv? Wake up."

Drawing in a deep breath, she sat upright.

He slipped his arm from around her before she noticed. "Wait there." He grabbed the umbrella, jumped down, and came around to her side.

She accepted his hand and stepped down.

Holding her umbrella over them, he walked her onto the porch.

Granny Bradshaw opened the door. "Troy, come in."

"Thank you, but I need to get the rig back." He closed the umbrella and shook off the rain before handing it to Liv.

She took it, thanked him, and disappeared inside.

That had been peculiar. She hadn't railed at him or shown any displeasure with him. This new docile Liv scared him.

Maybe having worked a week would make her more amenable to his offer of help when he spoke with her tomorrow.

Olivia couldn't believe she'd fallen asleep in the buggy next to Troy yesterday. She did her best not to look at him today. Traveling to and from church and even at church hadn't been a problem. But sitting across from him at their dinner table was another matter.

She stood and collected the dirty dishes.

Troy stood as well and picked up two plates. "I'll help."

"That's all right. I can manage." She held her hand out for the plates he had.

He flashed his dimpled smile and sauntered into the kitchen.

Grrr. He was going to be difficult today. She would just have to order him out of the kitchen.

After setting the plates on the counter, Troy rolled up his sleeves. "I'll wash."

Her bluster left her. Her dry, cracked hands ached from extra laundry and packing salmon all week. She couldn't turn him down. He was making himself a blessing.

He shaved soap into the dishpan, poured in hot water from the kettle and slipped several dishes into the soapy water.

She was about to warn him that the water was nearly scalding, but he plunged his hands in.

She waited.

He didn't pull them out.

"Isn't that water too hot?"

"A bit, but I don't want it to get too cold before I finish."

Maybe it wasn't as hot as she thought it was. But still hotter than she could stand.

After Troy finished washing the dishes, he stood behind her and planted his hands on the counter on either side of her.

She faced him. "What are you doing?" His nearness caused her heart to speed up and her breath to catch.

"I need to talk to you."

"You can talk from over there." She pointed across the room.

"I don't want you running away from me."

Her anger flared, and she pushed on his arm. "Oh, let me go."

"Keep your voice down. You don't want your mother and grandmother to come in here. What I have to say is not for them to hear. It's for you alone. Unless you decide to tell them."

Mother and Gran didn't need to be unnecessarily upset. Olivia settled back against the counter and folded her arms. Let him think his nearness had no affect on her. "What?"

"I know why you took the job at the cannery and are taking in laundry and mending."

She straightened her shoulders. What did he know?

"Your father's money is gone."

How did he know?

"I thought he'd had enough to last the three of you for years. The rent on this place is due. If you don't pay, you'll all be out on the street."

How did he know all that? "It's none of your concern."

He gripped her shoulders. "It is my concern, because I love you." He paused, studying her face.

For an instant, she thought he might ask—no *demand*—to marry her. With small, tight motions, she shook her head.

He drew in a deep breath. "I have money in the bank and have made a few good investments. I'll pay your rent so you don't have to work your fingers to the bone and still not have enough."

He wanted to help them? But what would it cost her? He would feel as though he would have the right to make demands on her time and attention. While dallying with every lady who looked his way.

She stamped her foot and spoke in a whisper. "No. And you will *not* tell Mother and Gran. We'll manage."

He grabbed her hands and turned them over. "Look at your hands."

They were red and chapped. She pulled them free and fisted them. "They aren't so bad." But they would be in time. She would also get used to the pain in time. Wouldn't she?

"You fell asleep in the buggy yesterday. *For an hour.* You are so exhausted."

She swatted his chest. "You shouldn't have let me sleep."

Though he kept his voice low, it was tinged with anger. "Don't do this to yourself."

"I'm not doing anything to myself. I'm doing it for them." She pointed toward the parlor.

"But you don't have to. Let me help."

Tears burned her eyes, and she shook her head, more deliberately this time. "I need to do this myself."

"Why?"

She didn't want to depend on him or anyone else. The pain of abandonment when someone left was unbearable. She could depend on only herself. "I just do. Please go."

"That's it?"

She nodded.

He stared at her a moment before releasing her. "You are too stubborn for your own good." He yanked at his shirtsleeves to unroll them. "You are like an old mule sinking in the mud, refusing help." He marched out of the kitchen and through the parlor.

He didn't even reply to Mother's inquiry if all was well.

Olivia's unspent tears spilled over.

She wasn't stubborn.

She was…

She was…

She slapped her tears away.

She was *not* stubborn.

Chapter 9

On Monday, Troy sat in Nick's trap outside the cannery. Waiting. He had fidgeted in his office all day, debating with himself whether or not to give Liv a ride home. He knew she would be tired. But he also knew she would likely cause a fuss, squaring her shoulders and insisting she could manage on her own. He had a mind to let her walk. Then she would come to her senses and allow him to help her.

But here he was, waiting for her. He was still upset with her for not accepting his assistance. It would serve her right to walk home, but he couldn't bring himself to do that to her. He would do what needed to be done whether she liked it or not.

When the door to the cannery opened, Troy jumped down to intercept Liv. An overpowering odor of fish wafted out with the workers.

Liv exited with another girl much younger than she was.

He stood in her path. "Hello, Liv."

She stopped and tilted her head back to look at him.

Her friend stared at him, too. "Oh, my." She held out her hand. "I'm Sally."

Troy doffed his cap and gripped it with both hands to avoid taking Sally's hand. He didn't need that kind of trouble in front of Liv again. "I'm pleased to meet any friend of Olivia's."

Sally shifted her gaze to Liv, waved, and walked away. "I'll see you tomorrow."

Liv waved back but continued to stare at Troy.

He couldn't tell if she was trying to come up with a retort or trying to figure out what he was doing there. Or was she just too tired to speak? He held up his hand. "You don't have to say a word. I have Nick's trap here to take you home. You can either go nicely, like a lady, or I can throw you over my shoulder and toss you in. The choice is yours."

She took a deep breath and let it out. Then she stepped over to the rig, held up a limp hand and waited.

That had been easier than he thought it would be, without having to threaten to manhandle her a second time. He took her hand, assisted her up, and then settled in beside her. "You don't have to say anything." He snapped the reins. The trap lurched forward.

He was tempted to talk her into accepting his help and quitting the cannery. But he'd told her she didn't have to talk, so baiting her, though fun, would be unfair.

At her house, he stopped and helped her down.

She didn't immediately hurry away from him but stood, looking down. He was about to ask if she was all right when she spoke. "Thank you."

That surprised him. "You're welcome."

He brushed her lips with his to remind her whose girl

she was. She didn't resist or pull away. Nor did she lean into him as she normally did. She remained impassive. He supposed that was progress.

She turned from him and walked up to her door without looking back. Walked might have been too generous. Shuffled would have been closer. She looked as though she might topple over.

Why wouldn't she just let him help her?

Each day that week he drove her home in silence.

Each day her "thank you" became more and more tired, until Friday, when it came out as a sigh. This life was beating her down. He couldn't stand by and watch any longer. But what could he do?

The following Sunday at the conclusion of the service, Olivia sought out Mr. Ingers in the churchyard. She made sure Mother, Gran, and especially Troy were nowhere near her. "Mr. Ingers?"

The portly older man smiled. "Good day, Miss Bradshaw."

"I wanted to let you know that we have some of the money for the rent. We might not have all we owe by the end of the month, but we will have most of it." She hoped he would give them an extension. If not, she would have to consider asking to borrow money from Troy for what additional funds they required.

"No need to worry."

"Then you'll allow us a little more time?"

"That won't be necessary. Your rent is paid up, as well as next month's."

A moment of relief flooded Olivia before dread pressed in on her. "What—how—who?"

"Mr. Morrison. He asked me to go directly to him if there are any further issues."

"Why would you do that?"

Mr. Ingers looked taken aback. "He is a man, after all. You should be grateful. Good day." He tipped his hat and walked away.

Olivia fisted her hands. How dare Troy go behind her back? She *should* be grateful, but not after she had explicitly told Troy not to interfere. Though appreciative to not have the imminent worry of losing the roof over their heads, she was now forcibly indebted to him. Troy had acted without permission. Without consulting her. And Mr. Ingers thought that because Troy was a man, his actions were justified and he could do anything he wanted.

"You ready to leave?"

She spun to face Troy. "With you?"

His pleasant expression turned to concern. "What is it?"

She planted her fists on her hips. "You! You paid Mr. Ingers our rent." Would he now force her to marry him?

His concern turned to dismay. "I had hoped to be the one to tell you. I was going to bring it up at dinner."

She shook her index finger at him. "How dare you do this?"

"What do you mean, how dare I? I did it for you."

"But I told you not to."

"You are unbelievable."

"I've never been so angry at you."

"Even when you caught Violet kissing me a year ago?"

She couldn't believe his audacity to bring that up. "That wasn't anger—that was hurt. You cut my heart out. This is anger!" She stomped her foot on the grass.

"*You're* angry with me? *I'm* angry with you."

Liv glared. "Angry with me? For what?"

"For not coming to me and telling me how bad things were. For not asking me for help. For being so stubborn."

She had intended to ask him for assistance if need be, but he'd taken that option away from her. "It was *not* your place to see to our debts. I will pay you back every penny."

"I won't accept it. Anything you try to give me in payment will go straight into the Bradshaw account at the bank."

How was she supposed to be self-sufficient if he was going to do things for her? Without asking? "I don't need your help."

"Yes, you do. You may not want it, but you need it. Let me help you."

"Evidently, you don't require my permission. You've taken it upon yourself."

He straightened. "Yes, I did. For your own good. I won't stand by and do nothing while you work yourself into an early grave. Not when I have the means to help."

Tears burned her eyes. "I don't want your help."

He stretched out his arms. "Why not? Would you rather lose your home? Think about your mother and grandmother."

She was. That was the reason she had taken the job at the cannery and worked so hard. And why she knew she would need to go to him for help eventually. But she wanted to do it in her own time, not have it forced upon her. "I don't want to depend on you—on anyone."

"Why not? Because you think something is going to happen to me because your father died?"

She didn't want to think about Father and his failings, so she nodded.

"Nothing is going to happen to me."

She hated that he remained so calm while she battled every emotion inside her. "It could." Just the thought hurt.

"It's not."

But it could. Look at Mother and Father.

Troy drew in a slow breath. He must remain calm. If he allowed his emotions to get as heated as Liv's, that would only make matters worse. He took Liv's hand, and she winced. He gripped her wrist and tugged off her white glove. "Look at this, Liv. Your hands are so raw you can hardly move them." He hated seeing her like this.

She pulled her hand away.

"Now quit that silly job at the cannery. You don't need it."

"Silly? You think me silly? You can't tell me what to do."

He hadn't been calling *her* silly. Why must she twist his words? His previously well-controlled emotions boiled over. "And you can't tell *me* what to do." He threw up his hands. "There is no reasoning with you anymore. We used to be able to talk. Now you take everything I say and turn it around. I'm through, Liv. I'm through. I can't put up with your behavior any longer." He walked away, needing time to bridle his anger.

He stopped at the pump and jerked the handle up and down. If this were an open well, he would consider jumping in. The water flowed, splashing onto the ground at his feet, splattering mud on his boots. That's how he felt with Liv these days. He wanted to throttle her. And he would, if he thought it would do any good.

How had life gotten this way? All topsy-turvy. Less than three weeks ago, he had been euphoric and ready to propose. Now his life was utter chaos. He and Liv had never had a fight this bad before.

The stream trickled to a stop. He pumped again, cupped his hands under the cool water and splashed his face. He took several deep breaths to tame his anger.

Once he had control of his temper, he found Mrs. Bradshaw and Granny Bradshaw saying their farewells to Pastor Kearns. "Are you ladies ready to leave?"

"Yes, thank you." Granny Bradshaw stepped away from the back of the wheelchair.

Mrs. Bradshaw tilted her head back to look up at him. "Where is Olivia? I thought she was with you."

He moved behind the chair so he wouldn't have to face her. "I'm not sure where she's off to." She could have gone anywhere in the interim. "I'm sure she'll be along in a minute." But he doubted that. Liv was furious enough with him to walk around the entire island just to avoid him. And he hadn't helped by letting his anger get the better of him.

He pushed the wheelchair to the buggy, helped the two ladies in and fastened the chair onto the back. Glancing around the churchyard, he saw no sign of Liv. It would serve her right if he left her behind. Or maybe she'd already stormed off home.

He gripped the side of the buggy to climb in but stopped at Mrs. Bradshaw's touch. He looked into her concerned blue eyes and exhaled. "I'm going to see if Liv's ready to go. I'll be right back."

The gratitude on Mrs. Bradshaw's face told him he'd made the right decision. He trotted off and found Liv right where he'd left her. "Your mother and grandmother are waiting for you in the buggy."

She sucked in a breath and jerked her head, having not heard him approach. "Oh."

Her red-rimmed eyes pulled at his heart.

He opened his arms and stepped toward her. "Oh, Liv."

She stepped back, shaking her head.

He stopped. "Be reasonable."

"Because you're a man, you know what's reasonable? You know what is best?"

He didn't want this argument starting all over again. He'd just gotten his anger under control. "Your family's waiting. Now come along."

"I'll walk home."

He should let her, but her mother would be disappointed. And Granny might pester him as to why. He didn't want to explain this to them right now. It would be easier if Liv just came. "Your mother and grandmother expect you in the buggy. You *will* ride home with them. So you can either come on your own nicely, or I can throw you over my shoulder kicking and screaming. What's it going to be?" This threat had worked before. But the last time he'd said it in jest. This time he would carry out the threat.

She stomped past him.

"Good girl."

She growled.

He knew he shouldn't have said that but couldn't resist. She was being so unreasonable. Whether she liked it or not and whether she was angry with him or not, he *was* going to help her. He followed in her wake.

She ignored his offered hand and climbed up into the buggy, fighting with her skirt and stepping on the hem as she did. When she finally made it up, she sat to the far edge of the seat.

He climbed in and sat as close to her as he could because he knew it would annoy her.

She tried to scoot away but had nowhere to go.

He wanted her to know she couldn't get away from him. He snapped the reins.

When they arrived at her house, Liv climbed down before he could offer his help. She strode inside without saying a word.

After he assisted Granny down, she said, "I'll give Olivia a hand with dinner." She strolled up the walk and went inside.

Troy retrieved the wheelchair, placed Mrs. Bradshaw in it, and laid the quilt across her lap.

Mrs. Bradshaw reached back and patted his hand as he pushed her. "Did you and Olivia have another quarrel?"

This time it had been more than a little misunderstanding or disagreement. "You could say that."

"I'll talk to her."

"That might only upset her all the more."

Liv had never been this angry with him before. And he'd never been this upset with her. He had known his actions would set off her temper. To protect her, he'd been willing to take whatever she threw at him. And he would do it again. Mrs. Bradshaw had no trouble accepting his help. Why couldn't Liv?

At the bottom of the ramp, she said, "Stop here."

He did.

She reached back, gripped his hand, and pulled until he stood in front of her. "There once was a sparrow who had a broken wing. She hopped along, flapping her good wing, but couldn't fly."

"You're telling me a children's fairy tale?"

She gave him a silencing look that only a mother could achieve. "A man found the sparrow and took her home. He wrapped her wing so that it could mend. But the sparrow was afraid of the man even though he'd taken care of her wing, fed her and given her water. This made the man sad. He wanted her to trust him."

So this was a story about him and Liv. He wasn't sure

he wanted to listen anymore. He already knew Liv was afraid.

"The day came when the sparrow's wing was healed. Reluctantly, the man set her free. The sparrow flew away, happy to be able to fly again."

He puzzled over the story, wondering if he should call it quits. "So, I should give up on her?"

"No." Mrs. Bradshaw patted his hand. "A week later, the sparrow flew back to the man's house and perched in the tree outside his window. When the man came to the window, the sparrow flew away. That saddened the man."

Liv's lack of trust did the same to him.

"The sparrow returned day after day, each time allowing the man closer."

Liv wasn't allowing him closer. If anything, she was pushing him farther away.

"After a couple of weeks, the man sat under the tree the sparrow perched on every day. The sparrow watched from a nearby tree, fearful the man would capture her again. When he didn't, she came closer and closer. The man held something in his open hand. Seeds. Though hungry, she dared not take the food. But the treat tempted her day after day."

The quilt slipped from Mrs. Bradshaw's lap. He retrieved it and put it back in place.

She nodded her thanks and continued. "One day, she reached into the man's hand and took a bite. When his other hand came up, she flapped away. Finally, she allowed the man to pet the top of her head while she ate from his hand. Soon the sparrow stayed in the yard around the man's house, singing to him. When he left his door open, she would hop into his house, singing.

"When winter came, the man was sure the sparrow would fly away, but she stayed, shivering on his windowsill. She tapped on the glass, and he let her inside. The man and the sparrow were happy and grew old together."

It was a nice story, but real life didn't end like fairy tales. "So you're saying I should let Liv go and hope she comes back to me?"

Mrs. Bradshaw gave a heavy sigh. "You are as thick-headed as my daughter. Be patient with her."

"Haven't I been?"

"More patient than anyone I have known. My daughter and I are cut from the same old stubborn cloth."

Patience. How much more forbearing could he be?

"Her father being gone hurt her deeply. She still hasn't gotten over that."

He knew that. Liv had been different since her father had died. He wished there was something he could do to help her get over it. The only thing he could do was be patient.

He pushed Mrs. Bradshaw up the ramp and into the house, then parked her in the parlor. "Good day, ladies."

"But you aren't leaving? You must stay for dinner," Mrs. Bradshaw said.

He glanced up at Liv glaring at him from the kitchen doorway.

Liv was angry with him. Good. That meant she cared. He was doing what was best for her—for them all—so he would gladly endure her wrath.

"I'm afraid I have a matter that needs attending to." Like getting out of Liv's way so she could simmer down. She would be more reasonable given time. He dipped his head and left.

He wanted to talk to Nick, to see if his friend thought he'd done the right thing. But Nick always ate Sunday dinner at Felicity's. And George ate at Anita's. Which had never been a problem because he always ate at Liv's.

He returned the rented buggy to the livery and walked down to the waterfront to pray. He petitioned and petitioned but could hear no clear answer. He turned at the sound of clomping coming up behind him.

Pastor Kearns reined in his horse. "I'm sorry I'm late."

Troy hadn't been aware they had scheduled a meeting. "I don't understand." Didn't the pastor usually visit people on Sunday afternoons who weren't able to attend church?

"I'm sorry. The Lord sends me places sometimes, and I don't know why until I get there. I forget He doesn't tell everyone about these things."

"He sent you to me?"

The pastor glanced around. "You're the only one I see. I'm to tell you to trust the Lord's guidance."

Wasn't that why he was here? To seek God's guidance? Once again.

"The situation may not turn out as you expect, but it will be as God intends."

Did the pastor know what his situation was? "How will I know if the guidance I receive is from the Lord?"

"He's already given it. And you know. Trust that what has been put into motion by your actions is right."

"Do you know what my situation is?"

Pastor Kearns shook his head. "I don't need to unless you feel a need to tell me."

Trust in the guidance already given. The guidance he received to pay the Bradshaws' rent? Then he had done the right thing. And in doing so had put something into motion. "Thank you. I think I'm good. You have helped me tremendously."

"Then I'll proceed with visiting folks. Let me know if I can be of any further assistance."

* * *

As Olivia prepared the meal, Troy's words echoed in her head. *I'm through, Liv. I'm through. I can't put up with your behavior any longer.* She'd finally pushed him away.

After Gran prayed, Olivia kept her head down for a moment. Was Troy's departure for the best?

Mother put her hand on Olivia's arm. "What is it, dear?"

Draping her napkin on her lap, she raised her head. "Nothing."

"Whatever you and Troy fought about can be resolved."

I'm through, Liv. She shook her head. "Not this time."

Gran dished up chicken and dumplings and set a plate in front of each of them. "I've seen Violet Jones with her own beau now two weeks in a row. I don't think you have to worry about her."

She wished it were only Violet this time. Troy had done something far worse. "When you tell someone not to do something, shouldn't they respect your wishes?"

"Did Troy do something you asked him not to?" Mother took a bite of chicken.

Olivia nodded.

"That's not like him, but he must have had a good reason."

Good reason? More like a selfish one to make her beholden to him. She pushed a chunk of potato around her plate. "But shouldn't he respect my wishes?"

Gran spoke up. "He usually has your best interests at heart."

Did he? Or was it *his* best interests?

Mother swallowed. "This has obviously really upset you. Why don't you tell us, and we can all figure it out together."

Would that help? She really didn't want to apprise them of the debacle. They would likely side with Troy.

"Keeping it inside won't make it go away. It will only make you ill."

Gran took a swig of coffee. "I once knew a man who was very angry. He fell over dead."

"I'm not going to die, Gran."

"Are you God? Do you know how many days you are allotted on this earth?"

"Of course not."

Mother touched Olivia's arm again. "Does this have something to do with Violet Jones?"

Olivia shook her head.

"Then what? What has he done that is so terrible to cause this breach between the two of you?"

"I don't want to talk about it."

Gran stabbed a piece of dumpling. "I can't imagine that nice young man doing anything bad." She popped the bite into her mouth.

Olivia could take her badgering no longer and snapped back. "You think Troy can do no wrong. He could run you down with a carriage, and you would be singing his praises with your dying breath."

"Olivia! You apologize to your grandmother right this instant."

Breathing heavily from her outburst, she turned toward Mother. "She thinks Troy is perfect."

"I do not. But he's a sight better than most men in town. You aren't going to do any better than him. And you best stop all this nonsense before you push that man away for good."

"Too late, Gran." Olivia put her hands on the table. "He doesn't want anything to do with me."

Mother pulled her hand away. "What?"

Gran shook her head. "I can't believe that."

Olivia looked from one disbelieving face to the other. "It's true. He said he was through with me."

"So that's why he didn't stay for dinner," Gran said.

"What did the two of you fight about?" Mother asked again.

"It doesn't matter. I knew he'd eventually leave."

"Your father promised him your hand in marriage. He wouldn't go back on that no matter what. So tell me this instant what you fought about."

"And we all know what Father's promises are worth." Olivia couldn't take the nagging. Neither of them would stop until she told them, so she blurted it out. "Money!"

"Money? What about money?"

"He wanted to give us money for rent."

Mother let out a quick breath. "Is that all? We may have to borrow from him before the month is up."

"No need, Mother." Olivia slapped her napkin onto the table. "He's taken it upon himself to pay our rent."

"What?"

"What?"

Gran and Mother almost spoke in unison.

Then Mother continued. "He paid our rent for just this month...right?"

Mother would think that.

"Our back rent as well as next month's. And he told Mr. Ingers to go to him rather than us!"

Gran smiled. "I knew I liked that boy."

Olivia glared at Gran.

Mother put her hand back on Olivia's arm. "You will go at once and apologize to him."

Olivia pulled away. "I will not."

Mother's features hardened. "When a person does

something kind, you don't get angry at them. You must thank them."

"I told him not to, and he did it anyway. We can't depend on him. Or anyone else."

"He has proven time and again that we *can* depend on him. Whether you want to admit it or not, we need help. And if Troy is willing to assist us, we need to be grateful. *You* need to be grateful." Mother picked up her fork. "He is apparently the answer to my prayers."

"Mine, too," Gran said.

Olivia pushed away from the table. "Not mine!" She strode out back. A light rain had begun to fall. She sensed that Troy was the answer to *her* prayers, as well, but she didn't want to admit it. She didn't want him to be. She didn't want to depend on him. She had thought the cannery job was the answer to her prayers.

Once again, she solidified her resolve to not care for Troy. Loving him was too painful. She had other worries without wasting precious energy crying over him.

She covered her face with her hands, and tears broke through.

Chapter 10

The next morning, Troy stopped short half a block from the bank.

Liv stood near the entrance with her back to him.

Waiting.

For him no doubt.

Had she come to chastise him again?

Lord, why can't she see I only want what's best for her? I don't know how much more I can take. I want the old Liv back.

But he received the same impression he always did, patience, which matched the story Mrs. Bradshaw had told him yesterday. If the Lord was patient with him, certainly he could be patient with Liv.

He really wasn't up for another scolding first thing in the morning. He didn't know when he'd be ready to face her again. Maybe a day or two. Should he duck around the corner before she saw him? No sooner had the thought popped into his head than Liv turned around and saw him.

Had she sensed him staring at her?

No turning back now. He forged ahead and kept his voice level. "Good morning, Liv."

"Good morning." She shifted her gaze to the ground.

She hadn't smiled. But then, neither had he. Still, he'd hoped she would have smiled. Even that tight one that told him she was still upset with him. "The bank isn't open yet." She knew that.

She glanced at the door and squared her shoulders. "I didn't come for that."

He braced himself for a reprimand.

"I've come to apologize for my harsh words yesterday. I shouldn't have spoken to you in such a manner."

Relief sparked in his stomach. This was an apology rather than another reproof. "Does this mean you'll accept my help?"

Her jaw tightened. "I still wish to earn the money for our rent."

"I see." He sensed it wasn't fully her idea to apologize. No matter. She had come, which was a surprise in itself. He took her hand and placed a light kiss on the back of it. Still bent over her hand, he looked up at her. "I accept your apology."

She didn't pull her hand away. She shook her head, and a smile tugged briefly at the corners of her mouth. "We would like for you to come to supper tonight."

He straightened and feigned surprise. "Tonight? Such a last-minute invitation?"

She pulled her hand free and planted it on her hip. "Are you coming or not? I need to be on my way, or I'll be late for work."

Ah, there was the fiery Liv he loved. He gave a sweeping bow. "Tell your mother and grandmother I would be honored." He knew it was they who had initiated the offer. But he could tell by the softening of her features that Liv was pleased he was coming, as well.

"We'll see you tonight."

"I can't wait."

She headed off in the direction of the cannery.

That had been pleasant. Especially after a night of tossing and turning, wondering if he'd done right by paying their rent.

Liv was well on her way to forgiving him. Once again.

He sensed tonight was going to be a change for them. A good change.

He couldn't believe the lightness inside him.

That evening after work, Olivia couldn't believe the lightness inside her even as she scrubbed her chapped hands. She lifted one to her nose and sniffed, and then the other. *Fishy.* The smell had probably soaked in clear to her bones. There was nothing more she could do for them short of making them bleed. And Troy would be here any minute.

His helping them hadn't been the upsetting part. She'd come to the conclusion she would need to ask him for help. That he'd taken the decision away from her had angered her. She felt helpless. She hated that. But apologizing had been the right thing to do.

She dried her hands and went to her room to change out of her fish-smelling work dress. She put on the light blue one she'd worn on the Fourth of July and tidied her hair. She went back to the kitchen.

Mother and Gran had made a feast. Fried chicken, mashed potatoes and gravy, cooked peas with scallions in a butter sauce, fresh bread and a cherry pie. Olivia could tell they had chosen foods solely with Troy in mind.

Gran pointed a wooden spoon at Olivia. "You're sure your apology sounded heartfelt? And he's coming?"

Olivia had known that the supper invitation was a way they could be certain she had actually apologized to Troy. "He said he would."

"He's late."

Mother spooned mashed potatoes into a large bowl and spoke in a calming voice. "If Troy said he'll be here, he will. He probably had to stay late at work. Supper's not ready yet."

Gran left the kitchen. Olivia knew she was going to look out the window for him. She hurried back. "He's coming." She patted Olivia's arm and nudged her into motion. "Go answer the door."

The sneaky old woman. She could have easily waited at the front door and opened it for Troy.

Olivia stared at Mother for support.

"Don't look to me," she said.

Troy's knock sounded.

Mother smiled. "Don't keep him waiting."

They were both plotting against her. Olivia expelled a heavy breath to let them know she was onto them and wasn't happy. She headed out of the kitchen but paused by the hanging mirror to check her hair before opening the door.

Troy stood on the porch, looking as dapper as he had that morning. He didn't appear as though he'd worked a full day.

Unlike herself, who felt wilted. "Come in."

He doffed his cap and entered. "You look lovely."

She felt anything but. "Thank you."

"I waited for you after work to give you a ride."

That had been kind of him.

She hadn't considered he would be waiting for her. Her only thought was to get home and freshen up before he arrived. "I was released early. I'm sorry you troubled yourself."

"No trouble. I'd do just about anything for you." He flashed his dimpled smile.

And her heart reacted. She led the way to the dining table that sat on the far side of the parlor.

Gran put the bowl of peas on the table. Mother wheeled in with a large bowl of mashed potatoes on her lap.

Troy rushed over. "Let me get that." He put the bowl on the table.

"Thank you." Mother touched his arm. "Would you mind retrieving the platter of chicken from the kitchen?"

"Not at all." He stepped through the doorway.

"Olivia," Mother said, "would you fetch the gravy?" She obeyed.

Troy picked up the platter. "Looks like you cooked all my favorites again."

"It was Gran and Mother." She wished she could take credit for the meal. "I was at work all day."

Once everyone was seated, Gran said grace. She made a point of thanking God for Troy's presence before asking the blessing for the food. Gran wasn't even trying to be subtle.

Halfway through the meal, Mother broached the subject Olivia knew she would. "Troy, Olivia tells me you have been generous and paid Mr. Ingers our rent."

Troy set down his drumstick and took his time wiping his mouth with his napkin as though the comment made him uneasy. "Yes, ma'am."

"That was very kind of you. Thank you."

"You're welcome." Troy's face relaxed into a slight smile. "I was happy to do it."

After a moment of silence, Mother continued. "But I must agree with my daughter. You should not have paid our debts without asking first."

Olivia jerked her head in Mother's direction. *What?* She was agreeing with her?

His face tensed again. "To be honest, I thought of coming to you, but I felt compelled to take care of it and tell you afterward. I didn't want to give any of you the opportunity to turn me down."

"I see your point." Mother took a small bite of potatoes and swallowed. "But I'm afraid you have given far more than we can accept."

Thank you. Olivia was glad to see Mother understood.

Troy stopped in midreach for his glass and made eye contact with Mother. "As I told Liv, I won't let you repay me. What's done is done." He picked up the glass and took a swallow of water.

"I see." Mother remained calm and kept her voice tranquil, almost hypnotic. "But I cannot accept so generous a gift from a man who is not a member of the family."

An odd feeling pressed in the pit of Olivia's stomach. What was Mother up to?

Troy paused only a moment before answering. "And I cannot let the three of you be turned out on the streets with nowhere to go when I have the means to prevent that. I promised Mr. Bradshaw that I would take care of Liv." He picked up his fork.

"You also promised my husband that you would marry Olivia."

"Mother!"

Mother held up her hand to Olivia. "Hush now."

Troy set his fork aside. "Are you suggesting…?"

"That you marry Olivia? Yes. That is the only way I can accept your generosity. You would be part of the family. Any other way would be inappropriate."

"Mother, you can't do that!"

Mother gave her a stern look. "I can. I will. And I have." She turned back to Troy. "Since you long ago agreed to marry her, what do you say?"

"No," Olivia said. "He says no." She didn't want to be forced into this.

Mother's voice turned harsh. "Olivia, be still."

Olivia glared at Troy. He was actually considering the matter. But he wouldn't look at her. He kept his gaze locked with Mother's. The two stared at each other. Who would back down first?

"May I have a few days to consider the matter?" Troy asked.

"I wish I could. But we cannot afford the luxury. There are many preparations to make. I'll need an answer by tomorrow night." Mother spooned peas into her mouth as though they had been talking about the weather and not Olivia's future.

Olivia wanted to protest but knew Mother would send her out of the room. She looked to Gran, who shook her head, indicating that she wouldn't help. So Olivia willed Troy to turn Mother down. Olivia was a helpless mouse, and Mother the cat offering her up as a sacrifice.

Troy straightened. "The rent is already paid. There is no need for you to move out when you have no place to go."

Olivia smiled at Troy having called Mother's bluff.

Mother's mouth curved up. "I have relatives in Chicago. They haven't communicated with me since I married Mr. Bradshaw, but now that he is gone, they will likely take me back. Take us all in."

And she had called his.

After a moment, Troy pushed back from the table and stood. "I will give you my answer tomorrow night. Thank you for supper."

"You haven't finished your meal," Mother said.

"We have cherry pie." Gran pointed toward the kitchen.

Troy's mouth pulled up slightly but not enough to fully engage his dimples. "I have more pressing matters to attend to. Thank you and good evening."

Olivia shot to her feet and walked him to the door. "You aren't seriously considering this, are you?"

"We've talked of marriage before." He put on his cap and strode out the door.

She couldn't believe it, and followed him, stopping on the porch. "Are you actually considering this?"

He swung around slowly. "It wouldn't be right not to. There is a lot at stake. For everyone."

She clenched her hands into fists. "You are going to decide this is what you want regardless of my feelings."

"I'm going to analyze the situation from every side and decide what's best for all concerned." He kept his voice irritatingly level. "Not just for me. And not just for you. I'm going to set everyone's emotions aside. Including mine. And make a determination rationally."

"Rationally?" She jammed her fists onto her hips. "So I'm an irrational female?"

He huffed out a breath. "I don't know whether your gender has anything to do with the matter. But you aren't being rational at the moment. I will not let my emotions or yours be a determining factor in my ultimate decision."

"Why do you get to make this decision that affects me, as well?"

"Because your mother put this decision in my hands." He tipped his hat and strode away.

"Please, Troy, don't do this," she said under her breath.

He didn't look back but climbed into Nick's trap and drove off.

Olivia returned to the table. Before she could speak, Mother held up her hand.

"Not one word from you."

Even if Olivia wanted to say something, she didn't know what.

"Do you think he'll wait for you forever?"

She knew Mother didn't expect an answer.

Did she want Troy to say yes or no to Mother's demand? Confusion spiraled around inside her. How could Mother do this to her?

"Apparently," Gran said, "her pride is worth more than the man she loves."

The truth of Gran's words struck her. Was it her pride? Or was she protecting her still-wounded heart?

Troy returned the trap to the livery, saddled the horse he kept there and rode out to Nick's place. He wanted to go back to Liv, but he couldn't let her influence his decision. This responsibility was his to bear.

When he reined in his mount, he saw another horse tied to the hitching rail. He dismounted, looped his horse's reins around the rail and knocked on the door.

Nick answered and invited him in. "Tonight's my night for company. Coffee?"

"Sure."

George sat at Nick's table with a cup of coffee in his hand and his feet up. "Howdy."

Good. He could get advice from both Nick and George. He sat across from George.

Nick set a mug in front of Troy and sat at the end of the table. "You look a bit…a bit like…"

"He looks like he's come face-to-face with an angry grizzly bear." George took a swig of his coffee.

"Yup. That's it," Nick said. "Did you have another fight with Olivia?"

Troy nodded and took a drink of the strong swill Nick claimed was coffee. "After church yesterday."

"Violet again?"

Troy shook his head. "She found out I paid their rent."

George shook his head, too. "That girl should be grateful. But that still don't account for you looking ill."

Nick nodded. "So what is it?"

"This time was different. Liv was different. Like she didn't care anymore. I didn't know how I was going to get her to forgive me."

"Boring." George stood and refilled his cup. "This is the same sad song you've been playing for a long time."

Not quite. This one had an unexpected verse. "Liv was waiting for me before the bank opened this morning. She apologized and invited me to supper."

"She apologized?" Nick's eyes widened. "Without you asking her to? Did you go?"

"I knew her mother and grandmother put her up to it. Both the apology and the invitation." But it showed progress. He wasn't about to miss a chance to mend things between him and Liv. "I went."

"Did something happen at supper?" George sat and swung his feet back up onto the table.

Troy snatched up his cup to keep the coffee from sloshing over. "You could say that. Mrs. Bradshaw said she can't accept my paying their rent because I'm not a family member. She said the only way she can agree to my assistance is if I marry Olivia, because then I'll be part of the family."

George choked on his coffee and clomped his feet to the floor. "Mrs. Bradshaw?"

Nick stared at Troy.

Troy nodded and went on. "If I don't marry Liv, they will all move to Chicago to live with some relatives there." Though he wasn't sure if there really were relatives or if that was a pretense.

Nick continued to stare mutely.

"Say something."

Nick shrugged. "I don't understand."

What? Was he daft? "It's simple. If I don't marry Liv, they'll move. To Chicago!"

"That part I understand."

"Then what? Was I wrong to pay their rent?"

George glanced at Nick and shrugged. "He's hopeless."

Nick tapped his skull. "Maybe he has a concussion or something."

"Maybe Olivia beaned him with a rolling pin."

Troy shook his head. These two dunderheads were no help. "I didn't hit my head. I want to know what to do. I have until tomorrow evening to give Mrs. Bradshaw my answer."

George opened his mouth to speak.

But Nick stopped him with a wave of his hand and shifted in his chair to more directly face Troy. "So your question is whether or not you should marry Olivia?"

Good. Maybe now he would get some straight advice. Troy nodded.

"The same Olivia you've wanted to marry for four years or more? The girl you've been in love with forever? The lady whose finger fits the ring in your pocket?"

Troy put his hand over the bulge in his vest.

Nick continued. "So your question is, given this perfect opportunity to marry Olivia Bradshaw, should you marry the lady you love?"

Troy nodded.

"Nope. You should move to South America and be miserable in some native village and possibly catch some terrible disease and waste away, lonely and in pain."

George nodded his agreement. "Yup. That's what you should do."

These two were of no use. "My mistake. I thought one or both of you could be the least bit helpful."

"We don't understand your dilemma. You want to marry Olivia, and here you have the perfect opportunity." Nick pointed to the floor in front of Troy's boots. "Laid right at your feet. Only a fool would turn her down."

"But would it be wrong to marry her this way? She was *not* happy with her mother's edict."

Nick leaned back in his chair. "Haven't you been praying—haven't we *aaall* been praying—for the circumstances to be right so that you could marry her? This sounds like an answer to all our prayers."

"Amen." George raised his cup. "I think it would be wrong to let her move to Chicago. Could you live with that?"

Troy didn't like the idea of her moving so far away. He would have to move to Chicago, too, then. He'd already followed her across the island from Roche Harbor to Friday Harbor. A big city couldn't compare with the lush green of the San Juan Islands. "What if she hates me for it?"

George waved a dismissive hand toward him. "She'll get over it once you are happily married."

Happily? He wasn't so sure.

Nick scooted his chair, scraping the legs against the floor, and leaned forward on the table. "Look. You want to marry Olivia. And she wants to marry you even if she won't admit it. So marry her. You have her mother's blessing. You even have her father's blessing."

"But is it the *right* thing to do?"

"Does that really matter?" George asked.

"A better question is," Nick said, "is it the *wrong* thing to do?"

"Nope." George shook his head. "Not wrong at all."

Nick glanced at George and nodded. "He's right. I'm sure Olivia will see it that way, too."

Troy narrowed his eyes. Liv would not see it that way.

"All right." Nick shrugged. "So maybe not at first, but she'll come around."

But did he want to start his marriage with her that way?

"Despite all her protests to the contrary—" Nick slapped his hand on the table "—she does love you."

Troy thought so too, but still…

The pastor's words from yesterday came back to him. *Trust that what has been put into motion by your actions is right.*

He'd paid their rent, and this was the result.

Chapter 11

Olivia's stomach had twisted inside her all day, nearly making her sick. She'd left work early again, wanting to remove as much fish smell as possible. Not that the odor would change Troy's answer. And what answer did she want him to give? She didn't want him to say yes—or no. She didn't want to be forced into marriage, nor did she want to move from her beloved San Juan Island. Especially to a big city like Chicago.

When Troy's knock came on the door, she jumped and sucked in a breath.

Gran smiled. "Go open the door for your fiancé."

Olivia thinned her lips. "We don't know that." What if Troy didn't want to marry her? She went and opened the door but couldn't read his expression.

He doffed his cap. His "Hello, Liv" wasn't in his usual teasing tone.

Her stomach tightened. "Mother's waiting for you."

When he entered the parlor, Mother sat in her wheelchair with her hands folded in her lap. "Welcome, Troy. Have a seat."

"Thank you. I'll stand."

Olivia remained standing, as well.

Troy twisted his cap in his hands. "Mrs. Bradshaw, is there anything I can say to talk you out of your decision?"

Mother drew in a slow breath before answering. "No."

He was silent a moment. He shook out his cap and then twisted it again. "Then I accept your terms."

Mrs. Bradshaw smiled.

"What?" Olivia still wasn't sure what she had wanted him to say. But she didn't want her entire future decided in this moment. Did she?

Troy dug in his pocket, lowered to one knee, and held out a ring with a blue stone. "Liv, will you marry me?"

He was asking? And he'd obviously come prepared. Had he purchased the ring today?

She looked from Troy to Mother. "What if I say no?"

"Then you have chosen Chicago for us all. It's up to you."

Olivia wanted to say no, though she knew she had little choice. But she couldn't bring herself to say yes. So she held out her left hand.

Troy took it and slipped the ring on her finger. A perfect fit. "It matches your eyes."

Tears stung. Happy or sad? She couldn't tell.

Troy stood, still holding her hand, which he wrapped around his arm. He spoke to Mother. "I thought maybe a spring wedding, or perhaps June."

Olivia stared at his profile, surprised he would give her nearly a year.

"I'm afraid that's unacceptable."

Olivia jerked toward Mother. "What?"

"Either the two of you are married by the end of the month or we move out."

Why was Mother being so persistent? Why wouldn't Mother give her time, as well? There was only a week left in July.

Troy's jaw worked back and forth. He took a deep breath. "If that's the way it must be, then very well. I'll talk to Pastor Kearns and see how soon he's available."

"No need. He's coming to supper on Thursday. He can perform the ceremony then."

That was only two days away. Mother had obviously planned for Troy to say yes. *What will I wear?*

"You'll stay for supper tonight?" Mother asked. "We saved the cherry pie for you."

He agreed. "I've been thinking of that pie all day."

Strained conversation dominated the meal. At the conclusion, Troy said, "Liv, will you quit the cannery now?"

He'd *asked*, not ordered.

"Of course she'll quit," Gran said. "Tomorrow."

Mother nodded her agreement.

"Apparently I have no choice in that matter, either." Her life was being ordered for her, and she was helpless to stop it. She stood and took her plate to the kitchen.

Troy followed with the other plates. "I'll wash."

She nodded and walked out the back door. She didn't know what to say to him. She couldn't tell if she was angry with him or not. A heaviness pressed in on her from all sides, as well as a lightness. It didn't make sense.

"Liv?"

She startled at his nearness.

"I'm sorry. I know starting our life together like this—forced—isn't ideal, but I do love you and will do all I can to make you happy."

She knew he would try.

"I couldn't stand the idea of you moving all the way to Chicago."

She had detested that idea, as well.

"I tried to put off the wedding. That was why I agreed to the arrangement. But your mother outwitted me."

Mother was good at that. "I appreciate your trying."

"Then you aren't angry?"

"No, I'm angry all right. I'm just not sure at whom or what. You? Mother? The whole situation? Father?"

"Your father?"

She shook her head. "Never mind." She did not want to talk about him. But some of her anger was directed at her father. This was all his fault. She was helpless in this situation, and it was his fault.

Troy trudged up the stairs of the boardinghouse. He wouldn't be doing this many more times. With each step, the oppression about his decision lifted. By the time he reached the door of his room, he was almost giddy. How could he go from guilt-ridden and sorrowful for forcing Liv into marriage to anticipation and exuberance in the span of a flight of stairs?

He'd tried to put off the wedding until next summer to give Liv a chance to get used to the idea and forgive him for his part in all this. But Mrs. Bradshaw had insisted. He was glad the wedding was so soon. That would give Liv less opportunity to try to get out of it. But he didn't like how she had resigned herself to her future with him. He wanted this to be a happy time for them both.

Nick and George were probably right that she would settle down once they were married. He hoped so.

He could hardly believe he was going to marry Liv. This week!

* * *

The next day, Olivia stood outside Mr. Ecker's office and drew in another deep breath. How would he take her giving her notice after working for only a little over two weeks? She raised her fist to the door and took yet another calming breath.

"Are you going to knock?" came a voice from behind her.

She spun around. "Mr. Ecker? I—I thought you were in your office."

"Would you like me to go in? Would that make it easier for you to knock?"

How embarrassing! He'd watched her stand there like a ninny, trying to garner the courage. "That's all right." She cleared her throat. "I came to give you my notice."

"You're leaving us?" He looked truly disappointed.

"I'm getting married."

"Troy?"

She nodded.

"So when you said you were done with him, you didn't mean it."

Oh, dear, he thought she'd lied. "No, I was. Or thought I was. It's complicated." She didn't want to confess to him that she was being forced by her mother to marry Troy.

"He said you just needed a little time."

"He did? When?"

"Your first week. He didn't like me lavishing you with my attention."

Was that why Mr. Ecker had backed off pursuing her?

"When are the nuptials?"

"Tomorrow."

His eyes widened. "A *little* time, indeed."

"I can finish out the week."

"That's not necessary. I'm sure you have a lot of preparations. Every bride does."

"Not really. We are having a simple ceremony at my house."

"Still, you'll have things to do." He opened the office door. "Come in, and I'll pay what is due you."

She followed him in. "You don't want me to work at least today?"

"That's not necessary. Have a seat."

"I don't want to trouble you."

"No trouble."

"Thank you." She sat. Her whole body relaxed, knowing she didn't have to work today.

After he figured the amount due her, he wrote her a check and held it out. "I hope you have a happy life with Troy."

She took the check but didn't look at it. "Thank you. I will." Why had she said that? She was being forced to marry. How could that be happy?

After leaving the building, she dared to glance at her check. Though it wasn't a huge sum, she felt good about having earned it herself. She should take it to the bank and deposit it, but she didn't want to run into Troy there and have to show him how little she'd made. She could take it to the bank another day.

She gazed at the blue stone on her finger. It sparkled in the sunshine. Her mouth turned up. Troy had put a great deal of thought into her ring.

Relieved at not having to work, she felt light as she walked to Felicity's. She hadn't told her friend yet about her upcoming wedding.

Felicity must have seen her coming, for she skipped out the front door and greeted Olivia on the walkway with a hug. "Is it true?"

How had she found out? "Is what true?" Just in case her friend was speaking of something else.

"Nick said you and Troy are getting married."

Of course Troy would have told Nick. Olivia nodded.

Felicity squealed and hugged her again. "I always knew you two were destined to be together. Will you marry before the end of the year or wait until next year?"

Olivia sighed. Obviously, Troy hadn't told Nick everything. "Can we sit on the porch?"

"Of course." Felicity looped her arm through Olivia's. "I want all the details, how he proposed and everything." On the porch, she released Olivia. "The water's hot. I'll make us a quick cup of tea. You wait here." She dashed inside.

Olivia sat on the bench swing at the far end of the porch.

Poor Felicity. She would be disappointed when she found out there was no romance in the proposal or the impending wedding.

Though Olivia was none too pleased at being forced to marry Troy, she also had a sense of security. As though her future could potentially be happy. But how could it when the marriage was under duress? On both sides. Mother and Father had married under good terms, and Father hadn't bothered to stick around. Would Troy?

Felicity returned with two cups on saucers. "I told Mother this was a special occasion, so she's letting us use the good dishes."

Olivia took a cup and saucer with pink roses on it.

Careful not to spill, Felicity gently sat next to her on the bench swing. "Obviously, everything's fine between the two of you again."

Would it ever be fine under these conditions? "Not exactly."

Felicity's smile fell. "But you're marrying him."

Olivia bit her bottom lip and then told Felicity the whole story.

"So your mother is forcing you to marry Troy, even though he's willing to help without marrying you?"

"Yes. Can you believe that?"

Felicity smiled. "I never would have guessed your mother could be so shrewd."

"What do you mean? You seem happy about this."

"I am happy. Your mother is using this situation to get you to marry Troy."

Wasn't that what she'd just told her friend?

"Livia, we all know you love Troy and that you are too afraid to marry him because your father left. Your mother wants you to be happy."

"So happy she is forcing me to marry against my will? How does that lead to happiness?"

"She's forcing you to marry the man you love because you can't do it on your own. She knows you love Troy and will be happy. Admit it. You still love him."

She did. "But what if I don't trust him?"

"It's your father you don't trust."

"But Troy is just like him."

"No, he's not. Troy has stayed. He hasn't left. He loves you."

"What if something happens to me like happened to my mother? He'll leave just like my father did."

"He won't. He's proven he'll stay. Now, no more excuses. We have a wedding to plan. Are you going to get married this year or next?"

Olivia's mouth pulled up on one side. "This."

Felicity clapped with delight. "How soon?"

"Soon."

Her friend's eyes widened. "In the autumn?"

"Sooner."

"Next month?"

"Sooner?"

Felicity's mouth hung open. "How much sooner?"

"Tomorrow. You'll come, won't you?"

Felicity squealed. "Come? You couldn't keep me away. I'll be over this afternoon to help in any way I can."

After Olivia's visit with Felicity, she walked home.

"You've returned sooner than we expected," Mother said. "We thought you'd have to work all day."

"Mr. Ecker was kind enough to let me go immediately. I stopped over at Felicity's. She'll be by this afternoon to help. And she'll definitely be here tomorrow for the...ceremony."

"Well, of course you'd want her here. Anyone else?"

Olivia shook her head. She wasn't interested in having a lot of people witness the distressing event.

"I'm sure Troy will want his friends here," Gran said.

"Yes," Mother said. "After the noon meal, go to the bank and find out who he wants to come. We will make sure we have enough food for everyone. Better yet, prepare a basket and take it to him. You two can eat together."

Olivia was both thrilled at the idea and repelled by it. But she packed the food and headed off to the bank. She tilted her hand again and again to make the blue stone sparkle in the sunlight.

Troy had indeed put a great deal of thought in his choosing of this ring. And how had he managed to get it to fit her finger so perfectly?

Chapter 12

When Troy's office door pushed open, he looked up.

With no invitation or announcement, Hewitt Raines entered, closed the door and sat himself in the chair across the desk from Troy. "We have a problem."

Troy doubted that he was involved in Mr. Raines's problem, but he had no doubt that Mr. Raines likely had trouble.

Hewitt held up his hand with a small space between his thumb and index finger. "There's a slight problem with Violet."

Oh, no. Not the day before he was to marry Liv. He would not let himself get caught up in Violet and Hewitt's troubles. "Miss Jones is your concern, not mine."

"Possibly not."

"Whatever it is, keep me out of it."

"You are already in it."

Troy gritted his teeth. "What have you done? And why have you involved me?"

"Violet found out about a certain incident with another young lady yesterday. She was furious. I might have implied I'd be highly jealous if she went back to you."

Hewitt was incorrigible. And Violet would likely seek Troy out to make Hewitt jealous.

Troy took a controlled breath. "It's been no more than two and a half weeks since you made up with her the last time. Why would you risk being caught even looking at another woman?" He knew he was talking as much to himself as to Hewitt. But Troy's encounters were purely innocent. Were Hewitt's?

"It really wasn't my fault."

Troy doubted that.

"Violet and her mother were off making wedding plans, and Mr. Jones had a meeting. I took the opportunity to stroll about town. I ran into a pretty little lady in distress." Hewitt held his hands out palms up. "Being a gentleman, I helped her out."

"I doubt that innocently helping someone would cause Miss Jones to be so upset with you."

"I ended up escorting her home." Mr. Raines wiggled his eyebrows up and down. "I accidentally kissed her."

Accidentally? Doubtful. "This is not a big city. If any friend of the Joneses saw you, or one of their staff, the word would quickly get back to Miss Jones. How could you not realize that?"

"I realize it now."

"I will not let you or Miss Jones pull me into this matter."

"She may not give you a choice."

"I am marrying my ladylove on the morrow." Troy stood and came around his desk. "Miss Jones will have to find someone else to make you appear jealous." He opened the door to let Mr. Raines know he was dismissed.

Hewitt stood and tipped his head. "I am glad to know that you truly have no interest in my girl. But that doesn't mean she has no interest in you."

Violet would just have to get over it.

"I suggest William Ecker or Titus Berg as suitable rivals."

Mr. Raines chuckled. "I don't think it would do for me to choose my own rival. Rest assured, Violet will be coming to you to get back at me."

Troy would have to make sure Violet couldn't find him. He saw Liv standing a few feet away at the same time Mr. Raines apparently did.

Liv held a basket covered with a blue-checkered cloth.

Hewitt swept up Liv's free hand.

Troy quickly stepped forward and retrieved Liv's hand before the man could kiss it. "I respectfully request that you not accost my fiancée."

Hewitt bowed to Liv. "Then you must be Miss Bradshaw. I am pleased to finally make your acquaintance. I can see why Mr. Morrison is protective of you. You are as beautiful as a bouquet of lilies."

Could this man not help flirting with every woman in sight?

"Good day, Mr. Raines." Troy escorted Liv into his office and shut the door. "To what do I owe the honor of this visit?"

Liv stood ramrod straight with both hands clutching the basket handle. "Mother wanted to know whom you'd like to invite tomorrow night. I assume Nick and George. Anyone else?"

So she had been sent. He'd hoped she'd come of her own accord. "Nick and George will be sufficient." The Bradshaws' house wouldn't hold many. "What's in the basket? Anything for me?"

The basket shot out on stiff arms. "Lunch."

He took it. "Thank you." She looked ready to bolt. "You'll join me, won't you?" He motioned to the chair, hoping she would stay.

She stepped in front of the chair, started to lower herself and then straightened. "What did Mr. Raines mean by 'Violet will be coming to you'?"

So she had heard.

He set the basket on the desk. "Mr. Raines had a disagreement with Violet. He believes she will try to use me again to make him jealous."

Liv stared, a question in her eyes.

He took her hand. "I won't let her. I promise."

"Even if it means your job?"

"It won't come to that. I'll tell her I'm spoken for."

"Why didn't you tell her that all the other times?"

That was a good question. "I don't know. Maybe I thought you'd find me more appealing if you knew other women found me desirable. Or maybe I thought you'd cling all the more tightly to me if you thought two or three women were waiting on the side. But I realize that thinking was wrong."

"Maybe you just like all the attention."

He did like the attention. But not at the expense of Liv. Not anymore.

She stepped over to the door.

He followed. "Aren't you staying to eat?"

She shook her head. "I need to let Mother know who is coming. Enjoy the food." She reached for the knob.

He put his hand over hers and turned her face toward him. "Liv, I love you. Only you."

"*That* has never been in question." Tears glistened in her eyes, and her lower lip trembled.

"My fidelity." His eyes had been opened with William

Ecker's interest in Liv, as well as Hewitt Raines's indiscretions that had involved Troy. "I will gladly spend the rest of my life proving myself to you." He caressed her cheek. "I will do nothing to make you sorry for marrying me."

"I hope so."

Olivia took her time walking home. She had much to consider. Which did she want more? Troy's love or his unwavering fidelity? To stay on San Juan Island or to protect her heart? Would marrying Troy settle the matter with Violet once and for all?

Lord, what should I do?

She had given her pledge to marry Troy. Wasn't it what everyone wanted? Troy, Mother, Gran. And herself? It wouldn't be right to back out after giving her word. And it didn't feel wrong to marry him. She wasn't sure if it was right, but it wasn't wrong. Which made no sense even to her. She would marry Troy for better or for worse, and that was the end of it. She hoped it wasn't for worse.

After she had greeted Mother and Gran in the parlor, she brought out two dresses.

She had let herself get distracted by Troy and had forgotten to figure out which one of her dresses to wear for the ceremony. The blue cotton one Troy liked or the pink one she liked? Mother and Gran would help her choose the right one.

Mother gave a knowing smile and nodded at Gran. Gran brought out a cream-and-white silk dress. Mother said, "I thought you might like to wear mine."

Olivia touched the soft fabric. "You had a white wedding dress?" More ladies these days were wearing white for their weddings, but not as many when her parents married.

"I thought about refashioning it after you were born, but my heart said to save it for you. I'm glad I did."

Gran draped the dress over Olivia's arms and waved her hand. "Go put it on so we can start in on the alterations."

Olivia stared at the dress that had not given Mother a happy ending to her marriage.

"What's wrong? Don't you like it? You won't hurt my feelings if you don't want to wear it."

"It's not that. You wore this dress, and look what happened."

"Nonsense. The dress had nothing to do with how things turned out. It was strength of character your father lacked."

Did Troy have strength of character?

"Yes," Mother said, reading her mind. "Troy's character is strong enough to withstand anything in your future."

"How can you be sure?"

Gran spoke up. "Even though your father was my own flesh and blood, Eugene was weak-willed. It was your mother who made him strong. She held him up. I tried to warn her off him, but she wouldn't listen. Troy holds himself up. He will do right by you."

Olivia remembered subtle comments between Mother, Father, and Gran over the years. Now they made sense.

"Would you like to try the dress on?" Mother's expression held anticipation.

"I'll be right back out." Olivia went to her room and laid the dress out on her bed.

Mother was right. The dress held no power over the future. She tried the dress on and went back out to the parlor.

"What do you think?" Olivia turned around in place.

Mother sucked in a breath. "You look beautiful."

Olivia felt beautiful in it and hoped Troy would like it.

Gran clapped her hands. "Let's get busy turning it into *your* wedding dress. We have a lot to do before tomorrow."

Tomorrow. Olivia would be Mrs. Troy Morrison. That both thrilled and terrified her. Her future would be set with him until death did they part. For better or worse.

Or until Troy left her as Father had done to Mother.

Chapter 13

Troy sat behind his desk on Thursday afternoon. Though he shuffled papers around, no work was actually getting accomplished. His thoughts were on this evening. His wedding to Liv. Had she figured some way to put off the wedding? Cancel it altogether? Or would Violet do something to spoil things?

With his door ajar only a few inches, he could see the bank's large interior clock. Still too much time for his nerves. He wished it was closing time. Once he was at the Bradshaws' and knew the wedding would still happen, he would be more at ease. He'd had a difficult time sleeping the past two nights because of his excitement about marrying Liv.

Finally, after all these years, she would be his.

He startled when his office door pushed open.

Jack didn't stay in the doorway as he usually did but strode up to the desk. He cocked his thumb to point behind him. "A man's here to see Mr. Jones. But Mr. Jones is out. Don't know when he'll be back. What should I tell him?"

"What man?" Surely, Friday Harbor wasn't so big that Jack wouldn't know who the gentleman was.

Jack's shoulders rose toward his ears. "Some fancy gent."

"Show him in here." Troy stood and straightened his jacket.

Jack darted out and returned a moment later. "Right in here, sir."

A man in his midthirties dressed in an expensive gray suit stepped in, carrying a suitcase and satchel in one hand, his hat in the other.

Troy moved out from behind his desk and proffered his hand. "I'm Troy Morrison, assistant to the manager."

The man shifted his hat to the same hand with his satchel and shook Troy's hand. "Ulysses Perrault, Esquire."

An attorney. "Please have a seat. Mr. Jones is out at the moment. May I be of some assistance?"

Mr. Perrault set his suitcase and satchel down and took the chair. "I would appreciate it if you could. I've been from one end of this...*remote* island to the other and now back again. Travel would be much easier and faster if you had a train running from end to end."

Troy sensed the man had wanted to use a description like backwoods or middle of nowhere. Not everyone appreciated the lush forests of the islands. "How may I help you?"

"I'm seeking a woman."

"Sir, women are in short supply this far west. You won't find one around here that two or three men don't have their eye on."

Mr. Perrault smiled at Troy's teasing. "Then good thing I'm not after a wife."

Troy was pleased at his success in relaxing the up-tight man. "So who is it you need to find? I know most everyone in town."

"I had thought to seek out an attorney's office but saw the bank first. I figured if you couldn't help and there was no attorney, I could inquire at the church. Hopefully you will have the information I require, and I won't have to remain on this wild island any longer than necessary to complete my business."

Wild island. Troy liked the sound of that. "Our local attorney is away at the moment. I'd be glad to help. If you will give me a name, I'll see what I can do."

"Caroline Tisdale."

Troy searched his memory. The name wasn't familiar at all. "I don't recognize that name. Let me look in our records." Most people in Friday Harbor had an account, and this one could be before his time here. He pulled a ledger off the shelf behind him and flipped through the pages. He pulled another record book from the shelf. Then he searched the file cabinet. No one with the last name Tisdale. "I'll be right back." He went through the files and ledgers in Mr. Jones's office. He returned. "I can't find any record of any person or persons with the surname Tisdale."

Mr. Perrault put on a pair of reading glasses, unbuck-led his satchel and pulled out a sheaf of papers. He shuf-fled through them and ran his finger down one of the pages. "Do you know a Eugene Bradshaw?"

Liv's father? "Mr. Bradshaw passed away two years ago."

Mr. Perrault's face brightened. "Then he did live here?"

"Yes."

"Married?"

"Yes. He's survived by his mother, wife and daughter."

Mr. Perrault expelled a long breath. "Then I am in the right town. His wife's name is Caroline?"

Of course. Troy hadn't made the connection. "Mrs. Bradshaw's first name is Caroline."

"And her maiden name was Tisdale. If you could give me directions to her residence, I would be most obliged."

Troy wasn't comfortable sending a stranger to the Bradshaws' without knowing more. Just because this man said he was an attorney didn't make it so. "As the Bradshaws' banker, may I inquire as to the nature of your business with Mrs. Bradshaw?"

"You would find out soon enough. I am here to deliver Mrs. Bradshaw's inheritance."

The air froze in Troy's lungs. "Inheritance? As in money?"

"Yes. I have a bank draft with me, as well as a few smaller items. I'm sure she will want the money deposited in your bank straightaway. Unless there is another bank in town."

"This is the only one. Is it a large sum of money?"

"I shouldn't disclose the amount until after I have spoken with Miss Tis—Mrs. Bradshaw."

Of course not. But this could alter his future. "Is it enough for her to live on for some years to come?"

Mr. Perrault smiled. "In a town like this? *Very* comfortably. Could you write out those directions for me?"

Money meant Liv wouldn't *need* to marry him today. Or ever.

Troy stood. "It's getting late in the day. I'm sure you're weary from traveling all this way, as well as across our island and back. Why don't I help you get settled in at the hotel?" He picked up the man's suitcase and clapped a hand on his shoulder. "You can have a hearty supper and get a good night's sleep. Then I will personally escort you over to the Bradshaws' first thing in the morning." After Troy had married Liv.

"That sounds marvelous. I wouldn't be able to conclude all Mrs. Bradshaw's business before the bank closed anyway. So I might as well start fresh in the morning."

By the time Troy returned from getting Mr. Perrault registered at the hotel, Mr. Jones had come back and met him at his office door. "I hear there was a man here to see me."

"I was able to help him." *Or at least defer him.*

Mr. Jones nodded. "Very good. I always feel safe, leaving the bank in your charge. Before long, you'll be moving up to manager, and I can return to civilization. I hear you are to be married this evening."

"Yes, sir."

"Congratulations." Mr. Jones shook Troy's hand. "Why don't you leave? I'll close up the bank tonight. And take tomorrow off."

"Thank you, sir." He hustled to straighten his desk and hurried out before Mr. Jones could change his mind or something could come up to delay Troy. Like Hewitt or Violet.

In his boardinghouse room, he had his meager possessions packed. He would take a suitcase with him tonight. Nick and George were going to help him move the rest of his belongings tomorrow.

He changed into his best suit. By the time he donned his coat, his stomach cramped so badly he had to sit down. The bed creaked under his weight.

What was wrong? He hoped he wasn't coming down with something. Not on his wedding day. Ill or not, he would go. He *would* marry Liv. He glanced over at the stack of six decorated boxes in the corner. He'd won her lunch box each year. And now he would have them for the rest of his life. If he could get to her house this evening.

Sweat gathered on his forehead and upper lip. His whole body shook and burst with heat. He jerked off his coat and loosened his tie.

He poured water from the carafe on the bedside table into the glass and took a sip. Then a larger drink. Feeling better, he shuffled to the washstand and splashed cool water on his face. Once. Twice. Three times. He stared at his pallid reflection.

Liv wouldn't want to marry him looking like this.

Then again, Liv hadn't been eager to marry him at all.

And now Liv didn't *need* to marry him. But she didn't know that.

But *he* knew.

And God knew.

He took a deep breath. He realized what he had to do. It was time to set the sparrow free. His stomach loosened, and he straightened. He changed back into his work suit and strode to the hotel. Hesitating at Mr. Perrault's door, he hoped the man wasn't there and knocked.

Footsteps thudded across the floor, and the door opened. Mr. Perrault stood in shirtsleeves and no tie. "Mr. Morrison, I wasn't expecting to see you until the morning."

Likewise, Troy had hoped not to see Mr. Perrault until then either. "I would like to take you to see Mrs. Bradshaw now."

"I understood we were going tomorrow when we could take care of all the business at once. Then she could deposit the bank draft, as well. Was I wrong?"

"No. Not wrong at all. I just changed my mind. With this kind of news, Mrs. Bradshaw would like to have it tonight. This will make her very happy. She will rest easier knowing she will have money in the bank tomorrow."

"Very well, then." Mr. Perrault knotted his red tie and shrugged into his coat. He picked up his satchel and followed Troy downstairs. "There is the will to be read and papers to be signed. I do like the idea of getting some of this business taken care of tonight."

Conversely, Troy didn't like the idea but knew it needed to be done. He held the door for Mr. Perrault. "It's not too far. Do you mind walking? Or would you like me to get a carriage?"

"I'm fine with walking."

Troy strode up the street with the man who was about to change his future.

And not for the better.

Nick and George exited Troy's boardinghouse across the street. Nick waved. "Troy!"

Troy stopped and waited for his friends. Mr. Perrault stopped, as well.

Nick gripped Troy's shoulder. "A bit eager on your wedding day? Afraid Olivia is going to back out?"

"No, things have changed. Nick, George, this is Mr. Perrault." He followed the introduction with a brief explanation of the man's business on the island.

Mr. Perrault had been silent, but now he concentrated his intelligent gaze on Troy. "You're getting married?"

"Not if what you said about Mrs. Bradshaw's inheritance is true."

"Ah. So her endowment will be rescuing you from an unwanted trip down the aisle?"

"Not me. My girl."

Liv was going to be vastly relieved.

"I see," Mr. Perrault said. "We can do this tomorrow."

"I think tomorrow would be better," Nick said.

George nodded his agreement.

Troy shook his head. "It has to be today. Now."

"Think about what you're doing," Nick said. "What this means. What you're throwing away."

"I know. I know." But he couldn't live with himself if he did it any other way. When Liv found out that their forced marriage could have been prevented, she would hate him. And he would hate himself.

After a moment of silence, Nick said, "If you are going to go through with this, you don't need George and me."

"No. The two of you best forget dinner, the wedding, or any other special plans for tonight."

"Are you sure?"

"Positive."

But they continued with him until they reached Liv's house. "Are you sure you want to do this?" Nick asked again.

George cocked his thumb toward Mr. Perrault. "We could kidnap this attorney so he won't ruin anything."

"I assure you, boys, that won't be necessary." Mr. Perrault turned to Troy. "It's up to you whether I walk up to the house today or tomorrow."

"This is the way it needs to be. It's the right thing." Troy thanked Nick and George and sent them on their way.

As Mr. Perrault let Troy lead the way, he said, "I don't know another man who would do what you are doing."

"And what is that?"

"It sounds to me like you are giving up marrying the girl you want to marry when you don't have to if you wait only a day. And now that you know her family will have a sizable amount of money, which you would be entitled to share in if married to the daughter, you are letting that all go."

He didn't care about the money. It was better when they didn't have money. But he did regret losing Liv. "This is the right thing to do." He knocked on the door.

Felicity answered. "What are you doing here? We weren't expecting you for at least another hour. Go away and come back later."

Troy put a hand on the door, stopping Felicity from closing it. "Mr. Perrault has business with Mrs. Bradshaw."

Felicity sighed. "Wait right there."

But before she could fully close the door, it swung open. Liv stood a step behind Felicity. "You're early?" Though her hair appeared to be fussed with, she didn't seem to be dressed for the occasion yet.

Liv was as beautiful as ever and looked as though she was almost pleased to see him.

He wanted to tell her it was all a mistake and take Mr. Perrault away. "A change in plans. There will be no wedding tonight."

"There won't?"

Troy took a deep breath. "Mr. Perrault has pressing business with your mother."

"Oh." Liv sounded disappointed.

But Troy knew better.

"What business?" Mrs. Bradshaw asked. "Certainly it can wait until tomorrow."

Troy had kept his gaze on Liv and hadn't noticed Mrs. Bradshaw wheel up with Granny Bradshaw. "This needs to be taken care of tonight so Mr. Perrault can be on his way tomorrow. May we come in?"

"Of course."

After Troy and Mr. Perrault entered, Felicity took Liv to the side for a few moments, and then she left.

When everyone was seated in the parlor, Troy properly

introduced the three ladies to the attorney. "Mr. Perrault has come all the way from Chicago. He is Mr. and Mrs. Tisdale's attorney."

Mrs. Bradshaw gasped.

Troy knew she would recognize the name. "It appears your relations in Chicago are no longer an option for you to live with. But moving is no longer necessary. Mr. Perrault is the estate's attorney and has brought you good news."

Mrs. Bradshaw gave Troy a look of sympathy. "So the sparrow has been freed."

He nodded.

Her next look told him she wouldn't have minded if he'd waited until tomorrow.

But that wouldn't have been right. He stood. "This is a personal matter. I can leave."

"Nonsense." Mrs. Bradshaw waved a hand for him to sit down. "You're family."

But he wasn't. He wanted to be. And he wanted to know if Mrs. Bradshaw truly had all the money she needed for herself, Granny Bradshaw *and* Liv to spend the remainder of their days in comfort. He sat back down, telling himself he was there only in an advisory capacity.

Mr. Perrault put on his glasses, removed a file folder from his satchel and opened it on his lap. "Mrs. Bradshaw, I first must confirm that you are indeed the person I'm in search of." She nodded, and he continued. "This first document I'll need you to sign is to confirm your identity. Please state your given name, place and date of birth."

"Caroline Louise Tisdale. Born in Chicago, Illinois, on March 31, 1855."

"Very good. And your parents' names?"

"Eugene and Louise Tisdale."

Dread in the pit of Troy's stomach grew with each confident answer Mrs. Bradshaw gave. He kept his gaze on Liv, whose gaze remained on her mother.

"Mother's maiden name?"

"Hillman."

Mr. Perrault handed Mrs. Bradshaw the paper and a fountain pen. "I'll need you to sign this as verification." He pointed to Granny Bradshaw and to Troy. "I'll also need the two of you to sign it as witnesses."

Troy turned to the attorney. "Me? Shouldn't it be Liv? I mean Miss Bradshaw?"

"She could…but you would be better, not being a family member and being a bank employee."

Liv nodded.

Mrs. Bradshaw handed the paper to Granny. Granny signed it and handed it to Troy.

He stared at the information on the paper a moment, making Mrs. Bradshaw's inheritance real. Did he want it to be enough to sustain them? Or a mere pittance so they would still need him? He signed.

Mr. Perrault put the signed document in the folder and then into the satchel. He withdrew another folder. "As your mother survived your father, hers is the will being executed today. This is the last will and testament of Louise Hillman Tisdale."

"Tell me what happened to them," Mrs. Bradshaw said. "How each of them died."

Mr. Perrault removed his glasses. "I think it's best if you don't know the details."

"I want to know."

Liv took one of Mother's hands and Granny took the other.

"Very well. The house caught fire during the night. Your father perished in the blaze. Your mother was found at the bottom of the stairs, unconscious. She was badly burned and had several broken bones. They surmised that in her attempt to flee, she fell down the stairs. She died the next day."

A tear rolled down each of Mrs. Bradshaw's cheeks.

Troy was sure the attorney could have conveyed more gruesome details. He was glad the man had not burdened Mrs. Bradshaw with them.

"I'm sorry for your loss," Mr. Perrault said. "Would you like to continue, or reconvene tomorrow?"

Mrs. Bradshaw shook her head. "Continue."

Mr. Perrault replaced his glasses and read the will.

Mrs. Tisdale's money was to be divided equally. Half was to go to Mrs. Bradshaw and half to be divided equally among Mrs. Bradshaw's children. If there were no living children, then the total sum was to go to Mrs. Bradshaw. Since Liv was an only child, she would receive the other half. The amount of money left to each of them stunned Troy. They could live *very* comfortably.

Liv really didn't need him.

Chapter 14

Troy took one document after another from the attorney and signed as witness.

Mr. Perrault shuffled papers around for Mrs. Bradshaw, Granny, Troy and Olivia to sign. "Because your father perished first, everything of his was left to your mother. Had it been the other way around, most everything would have gone to the university."

Troy understood. Mrs. Bradshaw's father had disinherited her. But her mother had not.

Mr. Perrault removed a cigar box. "As the will stipulated, your mother left you all her jewelry. I am sorry to say most of it was lost in the fire. I have a few pieces here that were at the jeweler's to be cleaned or repaired." He lifted the lid, took out a cloth and unfolded it on his lap. Inside were four white silk cloths. He unfurled them one at a time. First, a small brooch. Next, a diamond bracelet. Then, a sapphire necklace and earring set. Last, another larger brooch.

Mrs. Bradshaw took possession of them and handed Liv the sapphire set. "I want you to have these."

Troy gaped. "Are those...?"

"Real gems?" Mr. Perrault turned to Troy. "Yes. Every one of them." He turned back to Mrs. Bradshaw. "The house and its contents were destroyed. But the land it sat upon is yours. If you would like to rebuild and move there, I can help you make those arrangements. If you would like to sell the property, I can assist you with that, as well."

Liv's mother nodded stiffly. "This island is my home. I'll sell the land. I would appreciate you taking care of that for me."

Mr. Perrault retrieved another folder. "I prepared documents for any contingency in the event you wished me to take care of matters for you." After having Mrs. Bradshaw sign a dozen more documents, he patted his satchel. "The last order of business is the bank draft I have." He handed over the note. "It's only a small portion of the money you will be receiving. We can meet at the bank in the morning to deposit that and make arrangements for the rest of the funds to be transferred to your account."

He removed another sheet of paper and turned to Liv. "Miss Bradshaw, your money is still being held at the bank in Chicago. As we didn't know how many, if any, children existed, nor their names, we kept the money in the bank until arrangements could be made." He handed the paper to Mrs. Bradshaw. "If you will fill in the names of all your children and sign, verifying the information, I will arrange for your daughter's money to be sent to the bank here, as well."

After completing the information, Mrs. Bradshaw returned the document to Mr. Perrault.

He tucked all the papers into his satchel. "That is all

that can be done for tonight. We can convene at the bank in the morning to deposit your check and make arrangements for the other money to be transferred."

Troy realized that was his cue. "I'll come 'round first thing in the morning with a buggy to have you at the bank when it opens."

Mrs. Bradshaw held up her hand. "Not so early. Would ten o'clock be all right?"

Mr. Perrault agreed. "One more thing. Neither Eugene Bradshaw nor any husband in the future is to have access to this money. It's a stipulation of the will." He turned to Troy. "You'll see to that as their banker?"

"Not to worry. Eugene Bradshaw passed away over two years ago."

"Very well." Mr. Perrault latched his satchel.

"No, he didn't," Mrs. Bradshaw said.

Troy jerked his head around.

Liv inhaled sharply.

Granny Bradshaw patted her daughter-in-law's arm. "Let it lie."

"I can't." Mrs. Bradshaw looked directly at Troy. "Mr. Bradshaw left us for another woman. He couldn't handle my being stuck in a wheelchair."

Troy stared and then glanced at Liv.

She shifted her gaze to her lap as she nodded.

He didn't know what to say. "I don't understand. You said he passed away."

Granny spoke up. "That was all my doing. When he run off, I knew he wouldn't be coming back. I thought it best to save Caroline and Olivia the disgrace my son's leaving would cause them. I convinced them to keep it to themselves."

"I am as much to blame. I readily agreed." Mrs. Bradshaw waited until Troy made firm eye contact with her again. "I'm sorry we kept that from you. You, of all people, should have been told. My actions were inexcusable."

"That's all right." He understood why they hadn't. He felt their humiliation as well as his own.

Troy left with Mr. Perrault. He was stunned at the turnaround for Liv's family. They were most fortunate. But he wasn't sure how to feel about Mr. Bradshaw. Should he be happy Liv's father wasn't dead? He'd looked up to the man. Wanted to be like him.

A twisting in his gut nearly knocked the wind out of him. Mr. Bradshaw had left his family for another woman. Liv saw Troy talking to other women regularly. Though nothing ever happened and he would never leave Liv for someone else, he must look the same in her eyes. No wonder seeing him with other women upset her so.

He'd been such a fool.

When they reached the corner a block from the hotel, Troy split off from Mr. Perrault. Mr. Perrault continued toward the hotel, promising to see Troy in the morning.

Pastor Kearns strolled up the road. "Are you on your way to the Bradshaws'?"

Troy shook his head. "I just came from there."

"Is everything all right?"

For the Bradshaws? Yes. For Troy? No. "Yes. They have had some grand news." Troy swallowed hard and held his head up. "The wedding is canceled."

Pastor Kearns raised his eyebrows. "Canceled? I should stay away then?"

"Of course not. They're expecting you."

"Very well. You aren't coming?"

Troy shook his head again.

The pastor put his hand on Troy's shoulder. "I'm sure it will all work out."

"Not this time. I'm not needed now." Troy waved

goodbye and parted from Pastor Kearns. He wanted to go to the waterfront to sort out these turns of events and to pray. But his feet took him to the boardinghouse.

Outside, Nick stood from a chair on the porch. "You look whipped."

"That's about how I feel."

"I thought you might be staying for supper at this point. You want to get supper at the hotel dining room? Then you can tell me what happened."

Troy had no appetite, but Nick needed to eat, and he'd like the company. "Sounds good."

Soon they were at the hotel and seated with cups of coffee in front of them. Nick ordered a meal, but Troy passed.

Nick took a tentative sip of coffee. "Hot." He set his cup down. "So, do you want to tell me?"

"I think I've lost her for good this time." Troy took a swig of coffee, scalding his mouth and throat. He didn't care. He raised the cup for another round.

"Whoa, boy." Nick plucked the cup from Troy's hand and set it aside. "It can't be that bad. You've always won her back before. You can do it again."

Troy raked a hand through his hair. "She doesn't need me. Both she and her mother inherited enough money to sustain them all comfortably for the rest of their lives and then some."

Nick let out a long whistle. "Where did the money come from?"

"Mrs. Bradshaw's mother. The relative in Chicago they were going to move in with."

"To me, this all sounds like good news. They aren't moving to Chicago, and Olivia doesn't have to work at the cannery. Aren't those both things you wanted?"

There was more, but it wasn't Troy's place to tell

Nick about Mr. Bradshaw. "But she doesn't need anything from me. I should have been more careful and not let Violet use me."

"Violet has her own man. She won't be a problem anymore."

"She could be. Hewitt got caught with another woman. He said Violet wants to use me again to make him jealous."

"Don't do it."

"I won't."

"Then you'll get Olivia to come around."

It wasn't that simple. Now that Troy knew about Mr. Bradshaw, he wondered how Liv had ever forgiven him. "It's complicated. There's more to the story than just them inheriting money. Her father did something before he..." Troy couldn't say died now that he knew the truth. "Before he was gone that is keeping Liv from trusting me." Gone could mean dead as well as left. "I don't know if I can overcome it."

He'd spent more than a decade pining after Liv. Maybe what he felt wasn't love after all. Maybe it was just an old habit.

A habit it was time to break.

Nick narrowed his eyes. "I've never seen you this defeated. I never would have imagined it possible. But there are two things I know. Olivia Bradshaw loves you. And you could charm an angry grizzly bear out of killing you for stealing one of her cubs. So you can and *will* win Olivia back."

"You think so?"

"I know so."

Nick's confidence in him made him feel better. "Tomorrow. I'll start tomorrow."

The serving girl set Nick's supper in front of him.

Nick pointed to Troy. "Bring him a plate, too."

Troy nodded. His appetite had returned. "Would you do me a favor?"

"Should I ask what it is first?" Nick snatched up his fork.

"Would you pick up Olivia, her mother and grandmother in the morning at ten and take them to the bank? I'll be waiting for them."

"Sure."

"I'll go over to the livery after supper and pay Turner for the rental." That would give him time to get the paperwork in order before they arrived.

Olivia hadn't even begun supper when Pastor Kearns arrived shortly after Troy had left. She had been wrapped up in all Mr. Perrault had to say. As Mother and Gran had been. She made a simple supper, heating a jar of beef stew they'd canned last winter and the rolls that were already rising and waiting to go in the oven. In short order, they were sitting down. Olivia bowed her head as Pastor Kearns said grace over the meal.

Mother was the first to speak after the blessing. "You must forgive us, Pastor, for not having supper prepared when you arrived. We had an unexpected afternoon guest who brought us some rather surprising news. We got distracted and lost track of time."

"Think nothing of it." Pastor Kearns accepted a bowl from Gran. "I hope the news was good."

"Some was very good." Mother glanced at Olivia. "Some disappointing."

Olivia knew Mother was referring to the wedding not taking place.

"This evening," Gran said, "didn't go as planned."

"I ran into Troy Morrison on my way over. I was sorry to hear the wedding was canceled."

Olivia stared at Pastor Kearns across the supper table. The way he worded that, it sounded as though the wedding were called off altogether. "But it's just postponed, right?"

"He said there would be no wedding. He seemed definitive. Said *he wasn't needed.* It didn't make sense to me. I assume it does to you."

It did. She and Mother each had money enough to not only pay the rent but to buy a much bigger house and live out their days in comfort. So the necessity to marry Troy would never come up again.

So when would they marry? Ever?

As she lay in bed that night, her eyes refused to stay shut. She stared up at the dark ceiling. The cancellation of the wedding wasn't the relief she would have thought it would be. She finally acknowledged to herself that she was disappointed, deeply and profoundly.

She had wanted to marry Troy.

Being forced, she could have been absolved from responsibility for anything that went wrong between them. If Troy left her or did anything else unacceptable, Mother would be to blame.

And it hadn't been right to keep Father's indiscretion from him. Had that been an obstacle to her marrying him, as well? Probably. Now that it was out in the open, she felt freer to love Troy.

Poor Troy.

She should have married him long ago and found solace in his arms over her father's behavior. Now he probably wouldn't want to have anything to do with her. He would feel betrayed because they hadn't told him the truth from the start. And he was probably hurt that the only way she would agree to marry him was under duress.

She would talk to him tomorrow. Beg him to forgive her. Ask if he still loved her.

Chapter 15

The following morning, Troy jerked to his feet when Violet Jones barged into his office, declaring, "You have to help me." The bank hadn't even been open for fifteen minutes.

"Your father is in his office. He would be more suited to assist you." After what Hewitt had said, he didn't want to give Violet any encouragement.

She plunked herself in the chair. "No, it has to be you."

Troy eased back down, glad to have the wide desk between them. "I am really in no position to assist you."

"But you are. I know you didn't marry Olivia yesterday, so you are free as a bird."

"I still love her and will marry her."

"But not today, so you can help me. I need you to make Mr. Raines jealous. He has been dallying around town with other women."

Poor Violet. She could find a more devoted man than

Hewitt. "So let him go. Why would you want to marry a libertine?"

"He'll change once we're married."

That kind of man never did. "He won't. He will only break your heart in the end."

Tears pooled in her eyes. "But I want him."

Should he tell her what she wanted to hear, or the truth? "He's using you. Manipulating you. He wants to marry you for your money. He told me so himself. You can do so much better than him."

She was young, beautiful and wealthy. She would attract another suitor in no time.

She sniffled.

Troy came around his desk and proffered his handkerchief. "He's no good."

She took it and dabbed at her eyes. "But—"

"Violet, you have a lot to offer a man. Find one who will love *you* rather than your money." He took her hand and helped her to her feet.

"But that man's not you, is it?"

He shook his head.

She leaned forward and gave him a peck on the cheek. "Olivia is fortunate to have you."

He wished Liv thought so. He felt eyes on him and let his gaze travel beyond Violet.

Liv stared directly at him. She had seen.

He glanced at Violet and back to Liv.

No. Please, Lord, no. Not again. He was to start anew with her today. Start charming his way back into her heart. Not give her more ammunition to shoot him down with.

Liv didn't move.

He couldn't read her face. But it was something akin to shock.

Violet gave Liv a smug smile, then hooked her hand around his arm and propelled him forward. "You must tell my father what you have told me."

He would not let Violet manipulate him again. As he passed Liv, he pulled himself free. "Please wait for me. I can explain."

She still didn't move or say anything.

He just needed her to listen for a moment or two.

"Troy, dear." Violet sidled up next to him. "Come along."

He turned on Violet and glared. "I will be there in a minute."

Violet's eyes widened. She nodded and opened Mr. Jones's office door.

Troy approached Liv and was surprised she didn't storm past him or throw an accusation at him. "Will you come to my office?" He cupped her elbow with his hand. He knew she thought he was letting Violet use him again. But he wasn't. He wouldn't.

She didn't fuss, cause a scene, or refuse. She let him guide her into his office.

So far so good.

She took the chair he offered.

Troy didn't want to go. He wanted to talk with Liv. Could he put off this encounter with his boss and still keep his job? Violet was probably telling her father he'd snapped at her. His job might already be terminated.

"Go," Liv said.

He knelt in front of her. "Please stay here. Don't move. I'll be right back. Well, as soon as I can." He hoped this wouldn't take long. If he was fired, it could be real short.

Liv nodded.

"Thank you. I'll be right back. Stay right here." He straightened and backed out of his office. *Please stay.*

Lord, keep her here long enough for me to explain. He knew he could get her to understand.

By the time he turned away from his office, she was still seated in the chair. Would she wait?

He knocked on the open door and took one step into Mr. Jones's office. Violet sat in the chair opposite her father.

Mr. Jones wore a scowl. "Come all the way in and close the door."

He didn't want to do that. "I have a customer waiting in my office."

"Miss Bradshaw? She's hardly a customer."

Her family did still have an account here, even if there was nothing in it. But there would be later this morning. But what he needed to discuss with her wasn't business. It was all personal. He glanced back to see if Liv was walking out. He didn't see her. She had either already left or would while the door was closed. He reluctantly shut it and remained standing.

Why had she come now? He'd said he would call on them all at ten. Why did she always have to show up when Violet was making a scene? She wouldn't forgive him one more time. How could she after what her father had done?

He'd lost her for good this time.

Olivia sat in Troy's office. She had been the most foolish of all the foolish girls in all of history. She had allowed her father's betrayal and her anger to blind her. She'd been angry with Troy for so long, she'd forgotten how not to be. Misplaced anger that should have been directed only at Father. And now, like after the morning fog lifts, she could see clearly.

The smiles and looks Troy bestowed on Violet and all the other women in town were not the same ones he gazed at her with. When he looked at her, there was love. For everyone else it was whimsy and charm.

After ten minutes, Troy returned in a rush. "You're still here?" He looked so pained and yet so relieved.

"I said I would stay."

"But I thought you'd...get tired of waiting."

That was kind of him. What he really thought was that she would leave in an angry tirade. The anger she'd had toward him was gone, as though it had never been there.

"I was supposed to come get you, your mother and grandmother at ten. I arranged for Nick to pick you all up. Are they here, as well?"

She shook her head. "I needed to talk with you first."

He sat on the corner of his desk. "I can explain about Violet. She had a falling out with her fiancé. What you saw was her gratitude for helping her to see he's not good for her."

"I don't want to talk about Violet or her problems. Or any other woman."

"But I want you to know that there is nothing between us. I promise."

She didn't want the conversation to be about other women. Just about her and Troy and their future. If he wouldn't change the subject, then she would. "I spoke to Pastor Kearns last night. He said you called off the wedding completely." Had Troy had enough of her? Had he finally given up?

"I thought it best."

Best? Best for whom? She held out her left hand. "Then you forgot your ring." She hadn't taken it off. She didn't want to. Now or ever. If he was ending their engagement, he would have to remove it from her hand. The blue zircon stone twinkled in the light.

He knelt in front of her and took her hand. He ran his thumb back and forth over the ring and her fingers.

His gentle touch thrilled her. He stopped with his thumb over the stone and his index finger on the band underneath. For one terrifying moment, she thought he might slip the ring from her finger.

His gaze met hers. "I bought this for you. It's yours." He released her hand.

She didn't want the ring if he didn't come with it. Tears burned her eyes. "Why did you bring Mr. Perrault to our house yesterday?"

He knit his eyebrows together. "He came to see your mother. I simply showed him the way." He'd answered the technical question, but not the emotional one underneath.

"But you could have easily waited until today. We wouldn't have known. Why didn't you wait? We would have married, and you would have had everything you wanted."

He heaved a heavy sigh. "Not everything."

She willed him to say it. To say he still wanted her. She opened her mouth to speak but stopped at the knock on the door.

The office boy stood in the doorway. "Mr. Perrault is here."

Troy gave a soft growl of frustration.

Olivia smiled. He was adorable.

"Tell Mr. Perrault I'll be with him in a minute."

"What does he want?" she asked.

"We were going to get the paperwork drawn up so all you and your mother had to do was sign them. Then the process wouldn't take so long."

How thoughtful. She stood. "See to the paperwork. I'll return with Mother and Gran."

He took her hand in both of his. "Don't go. You are more important."

"I know." She patted his hand. "I'll be back."

He still didn't release her. "What you saw with Violet didn't mean anything."

It had meant the world to her. Her eyes had been opened. "We'll talk about it after the paperwork is signed."

He reluctantly released her hand. He probably thought she'd never talk to him again.

She left his office.

Mr. Perrault greeted her in the lobby. "Miss Bradshaw, how nice to see you. I wasn't expecting you until after ten."

"I had some preliminary business to discuss with Mr. Morrison. I will see you in a while."

"Very good. Until then." He ducked into Troy's office.

Troy gazed at Olivia a moment before easing the door closed.

She gave him an encouraging nod just before he disappeared from sight.

"If you don't marry him in a hurry, I *will* steal him away from you."

Olivia turned to face Violet. She felt absolutely no threat from the dark-haired beauty. How could she have ever thought Troy preferred Violet over her? She had to stifle a laugh at the absurdity of it. "You can try, but you won't succeed, so you might as well not even trouble yourself. In fact, Violet, I don't think there is a man in this town who could make you happy."

Poor Violet. She grasped at illusions she thought were love. She would never be satisfied staying on these islands. She was too big for them. The whole world might not be big enough for her.

"I think you should fish for a husband on the mainland. That is where you will find the man of your dreams."

Violet stared a moment and then said softly, "You think so?"

"I do. I think there is a man out there that is just perfect for you. But you won't find him if you stay in Friday Harbor." Olivia walked away, leaving Violet to contemplate her future.

Later, when Olivia returned with Mother and Gran and sat in Troy's office, she grew impatient. It was wonderful, certainly, to have a large sum of money deposited into her brand-new account. But right now, she had more important things on her mind. Her gaze slid to Troy, then back to her hands clasped tightly on her lap. Her knee bounced up and down. How many more pieces of paper would they need to sign?

Finally, Mr. Perrault straightened the last stack of papers, tucked them into his satchel and stood. "That should about do it." He shook Troy's hand and nodded to the rest of them. "Mrs. Bradshaw, I'll send you word on the sale of your property. Good day." As he strode through the doorway, the breeze of his passing fluttered the feather on Mother's hat.

Troy stood. "I don't think that man could get out of here and off our island fast enough."

Olivia knew the feeling. About having the paperwork completed, not about leaving the island.

Troy maneuvered behind Mother's chair. "I'll take you ladies home."

Olivia remained seated.

Once out of his office, he looked back. "Are you coming, Liv?"

"What about Nick?"

"I told him to leave the carriage and he could go. I didn't see any reason to make him wait around."

She stood and followed the trio out. She certainly didn't want to be left behind, not with unfinished business.

Troy settled them all in the buggy and drove them home. He helped Gran down, retrieved the wheelchair and placed Mother in it.

Olivia positioned herself for him to assist her, but he gripped the wheelchair instead.

He looked back over his shoulder. "You wait there for me." He pushed Mother up the walk.

Olivia was about to protest but realized Troy was as anxious for them to talk as she was. But she was too antsy to just sit and climbed down out of the buggy on her own.

Troy returned in short order. "I thought you were going to wait in the buggy. I thought I'd take you for a ride."

"Don't you have to return to work?"

"Mr. Jones gave me the day off on account of us getting married last night. Even though we didn't, he still said I could have the rest of the day. He was elated about your mother's deposit and the money that will be transferred later." He raised his eyebrows. "Buggy ride?"

She was about to accept and then shook her head. "We should talk first."

"I know what you saw this morning looked like there is something going on between Violet and me, but there isn't."

Olivia kept her voice level. "If you mention her name one more time today, I'll scream."

"I thought that was what you wanted to talk about."

She shook her head. "What I want to know is why you called off the wedding."

He took a step back. "You were marrying me out of

a need that no longer exists. It wouldn't have been right. You have money now—you don't need me."

She had thought she wanted him to marry her under the guise of a forced marriage. But hearing him say he wanted to do the right thing made her love him all the more. "Don't you want to marry me?"

"Of course I do. With all my heart. I had secretly hoped your mother's inheritance wouldn't be much and you'd still need me. But I don't want to start our life together that way. With you being forced."

"Then *ask* me."

He stared at her a moment before the significance of her statement dawned on him. But he didn't move. "If your mother or grandmother have pressured you into fulfilling your obligation because you agreed to marry me when it was necessary, you don't have to. I thought I wanted you no matter the circumstances. But I don't. I want to be wanted, too. By you. I love you and want your love in return."

"I do love you."

He swallowed hard, pain flickering in his eyes. He closed them for a moment.

She could see he was struggling. Didn't he love her anymore?

His voice came out hoarse. "Please don't say that because you think you have to. I know you don't trust me, and now I understand why."

Gran's comment about her pride being more important than Troy came back to her and stung anew. An ache twisted in her chest over the grief she'd caused the man she loved. "I have been angry at you for so long, I didn't know how not to be. But last night, I realized you weren't the source of my anger. The one I'm actually angry with is my father."

"I always thought he was a steadfast man. I looked up to him. But I will show you that I'm nothing like your father. I won't do what he did."

"It's true that I was afraid you would leave me as my father left mother. Left all of us."

"I would never do that to you."

"I know that now. I finally recognized what can be clearly seen in your expression. You look at Violet and all the others differently than you do me."

He nodded. "I care for you in ways I could never care for anyone else."

She liked hearing that. "I have no doubt of your love or your fidelity."

The worry lines on his face softened. "I will prove to you I'm worthy of you and hopefully you will truly fall in love with me."

Prove? That was what had kept them apart before. "You will do no such thing. I haven't the patience for that again."

"You won't even let me at least try?"

She stepped closer and took his hand. "I lost my heart to you when I was thirteen. You would come over to do chores for my father to earn money for your family. Then you paid me no attention until I was fifteen and other boys started noticing me."

"I got in fights with a couple of them over you."

"I suspected as much. But then you had the silly notion to prove to my father that you were good enough for me. He turned out to be the one not good enough."

"I thought it was your grief pushing me away."

"It was. My grief over my father not being the man I thought he was. But you are not him." She held his hand with both of hers. "You have nothing to prove to me. I love you."

He furrowed his eyebrows. "Do you mean that? Or are you just saying that because you think you are supposed to?"

"I really and truly mean it. My prolonged anger got you used to being on guard and defending yourself for so long, you forgot how to trust in us. Maybe it is I who needs to prove myself to you. I love you, Troy Morrison. I love you. And I will keep repeating it until you believe me. I love you."

A slow smile stretched his mouth, and his dimples appeared. Leaning forward, he cupped her face and kissed her. "I believe you. Welcome back."

It was good to be back. "Now, are you going to marry me?"

"Yes, my darling, yes. I will marry you whenever and wherever you say. Please say you won't make me wait until next year."

"Certainly not."

He raised his eyebrows. "This fall? Or possibly the end of the summer?"

"Perhaps tomorrow."

His eyes widened, and he kissed her again, long and passionately.

She finally felt healed and whole.

On Sunday, the sun shone brightly, warming the day. Olivia waited outside the church. At the end of the morning service, Pastor Kearns invited the entire congregation to return in the early afternoon to be witness to the blessed event. Unlike before, she wanted the whole world—or at least the whole town—to witness her marriage to Troy. Though they hadn't been able to marry yesterday, today was soon enough.

Mother had refashioned her dress into an elegant, contemporary style for Olivia.

Since her father was gone, Olivia chose to walk up the aisle by herself to show she was a modern, independent woman.

When she stood at the back of the church and gazed at Troy standing in the front, she forgot to walk and ran to him.

Affectionate laughter rippled through the crowd.

He clasped her in his arms and whispered, "The sparrow has returned."

She tilted her head. "What?"

He smiled, his eyes alight with amusement. "Nothing."

Granny called out, "About time!"

* * * * *

REQUEST YOUR FREE BOOKS!

2 FREE INSPIRATIONAL NOVELS
PLUS 2
FREE
MYSTERY GIFTS

Love Inspired®

REQUEST YOUR FREE BOOKS!

2 FREE INSPIRATIONAL NOVELS
PLUS 2 *FREE* MYSTERY GIFTS

Love Inspired HISTORICAL